DREAD

& THE

BROKEN WITCH

ANDREW WALLACE

LUNA NOVELLA #3

For Lana

Contents

A Wreck in the Desert

The Broken Witch lay by the wreck in the desert, planning tonight's mayhem and feeling beautiful. It was the tenth hour of day and the sun was testing its strength ahead of the burning time. The Broken Witch was naked, enjoying the way her dark skin drank the morning's power as she tried to remember where in the wreck, she had put the gugga ball.

The ball was essential for the Broken Witch's plans, which involved rubbing the resin against her gums until she started seeing things. She would then head to the village, which was an hour away, and on arrival be suitably altered in mood and perception to imagine she was hearing voices. Once that happened, she would lie in the centre of the village and shout at people.

After two hours of that she would pass out spectacularly, her body twitching and her eyes rolled back until only the whites showed. This activity usually drove everyone indoors, so when darkness fell the Broken Witch would be free to break into the Widow Ndugu's hut, making so much noise that the Widow Ndugu caught her. The last three times this had happened the Widow Ndugu, who was older than the

Broken Witch but much bigger, had beaten the Broken Witch's bottom for ten solid minutes and then pissed on her. The Broken Witch was hoping for more of the same; she adored running out of the village into the night, widow-fragrant and dripping, with her backside atingle. Descent from the gugga ball would then become a sweet flight across moonlit dunes into soft-woven darkness.

By the wreck in the desert, the Broken Witch breathed deeply. She was clean and the day was early, so she smelled of just-baked bread. Desire to preserve that delicious sense prompted the Broken Witch to get up, but she stopped when she felt movement in the desert.

Someone was coming.

The rhythm of their feet in the sand made clear it was a child. There was an eagerness to the movement, offset by a drag in the footsteps. The child had been running. Definitely a boy; they tended to overestimate their physical prowess. No one younger than eight would be allowed to journey out here, so the Broken Witch considered the village's nine-year old boys.

It was Togo, she decided. Kind, loyal Togo's head was full of dreams, some of which he told the Broken Witch about as only she listened. The Broken Witch thought Togo's dreams were wonderful and she was often in trouble for encouraging the boy.

The Broken Witch moved slowly to her feet and patted sand from her back. Approaching her fortieth year, she was conscious of a new stiffness, while her breasts had begun to stretch and her belly to soften. She didn't mind; to her, it was a new means of sensing things. She had even come to terms with her hair, monstrous though it was.

When she had gone north to the war that broke her, her hair had been a glorious black cloud: a tight-woven sphere whose bouncy contours demanded constant upkeep. Now, though, it was straight and shiny, licking down her back like a cross between the tongue of a monster and a foolish bit of cloth. It moved when she moved, got in her eyes and generally flapped about. Thankfully, there was little wind in the desert or the whole arrangement would have been intolerable. She'd tried hacking it off with the stonesung knife that had been her father's, but the hair always grew back. It reached the Broken Witch's backside in under a week and stayed there like a mockery.

She had considered burning it off but needed help to ensure she didn't harm her face. She had asked one of the men from the village to assist, but he'd got nervous and asked the Headmun for advice. The Headmun was angry with the Broken Witch and told her to stop wasting everyone's time. The Broken Witch shouted at the Headmun for so long she ran out of words and used noises instead, but it made no difference. The Broken Witch realised that although she didn't like her hair, everyone else did.

One of the women there said that the Broken Witch's hair was so shiny she could see herself in it. The Broken Witch had lifted the woman with one hand and tried to shake this nonsense out of her, but the woman looked down at the Broken Witch with a calm gaze and a proud chin. Eventually, the Broken Witch had put the woman back on the ground and asked her forgiveness. The woman had said no and flounced off.

Later, the Broken Witch had fetched some berries she'd been saving to bribe the Chief of the nomadic cattle tribe for a new wrap, now that the Broken Witch could no longer make wraps herself. She went around to the woman's hut and gave her the berries. The woman glared at the Broken Witch but accepted the berries and told the Broken Witch to kneel on the floor. The Broken Witch did so, head bowed. The woman stood over the Broken Witch and stroked her strange hair, saying 'beautiful' over and over again.

The Broken Witch had cried while the woman ate some of the berries and gave some to the Broken Witch. As the berries began to transport the two women deeper into themselves, the Broken Witch had reached up to the other's hips and stroked them through the orange cloth of her wrap. For a time, hair and hips were stroked and then the woman had unwrapped herself like a gift. The Broken Witch leaned forward and drank deeply of the woman, who began to sing and kept singing until the Broken Witch made her shake again.

The hair, then, had some things going for it although it remained the one part of the Broken Witch she saw as a questionable ally rather than an integral part of her loveliness. It wasn't surprising. The same catastrophe that had stripped the power from the Broken Witch's blood had blasted her hair straight. That she couldn't remember what had happened was possibly fortunate, but equally possibly not.

Her pubic hair remained defiantly curly and she plucked at it, checking for sand and finding none. She thought this absence unlikely and lifted her penis to check underneath. No sand there either. She lowered the penis again, regarding its length and attractively exposed light purple head with pride.

She could have changed it of course; when she grew her breasts, prettified her nose and eased the tough line of her permanently hairless jaw it would have been well within her power to fold the penis inside, create suitable openings and make her own lady piece. She had been powerful enough to grow a womb as well and considered it for long time, because she loved children and imagined one growing within her.

In the end, though, she knew herself too well; knew she loved the power, the ease and most of all the rude fun of the male sex organ so she kept it, as she kept her large, long-fingered hands: they pleased her and they were useful.

She loved women and men equally and they loved her, often at the same time. At an early age, she knew she would need some alteration to cope with the rigours demanded of her many appetites and so she modified her anus, using it for the passage of waste in one direction and loving pleasure in the other. It had a powerful elasticity, like a vagina but much tighter, and it never tore no matter how unrelenting her partners. It secreted a natural lubricant that tasted of honey; this latter detail proof to the Broken Witch in her many dark hours that she had been, and in some form still was, a genius. She called her man part the Black Lion and her lady part the Glory.

Satisfied that no sand clung to her, the Broken Witch reached for the strip of multi-coloured cloth that hung from one of the wreck's odd protrusions and began to wrap the garment around herself. She knotted it at the waist, wound it around her thighs halfway to her knees, drew it up through a fold and around one shoulder, under her breasts to support them, across them for the appearance of modesty and over the other shoulder. A second knot held the wrap in place, presenting the Broken Witch as a slim, improbably busty woman of average height whose high buttocks and narrow hips were not usually favourable markers of female attractiveness among her people, whose women tended to thick, powerful thighs, hips one could balance things on and big hair like the Broken Witch had once enjoyed and still loudly and irritatingly yearned for.

The wrap had one piece hanging down; this part of the garment had little pockets that were presently empty and a length that could act as a sling for larger items like the stonesung knife. The Broken Witch tucked the pocket length away for now and strutted around the edge of the wreck to meet Togo.

"Bambomiyi!" the boy cried.

No one called her the Broken Witch. Indeed, she was unsure if the village even knew she was broken. Since she had stumbled back from the war fourteen years ago, she had made do with remembered skills and knowledge to attend the village's medical needs, and sex, trickery and intimidation to negotiate everything else. As long as she kept safely delivering babies, healing wounds and seeing off disease they tolerated her, but of late she had been aware of a worrying loss of memory; a gradual slide into darkness.

The signs were there from the start; she could not remember her own name and even when they told her what it was, the knowledge would not stick. She tried to get them to call her Black Lion and Glory, but they weren't having that. There was no word for exactly what she was, so they'd borrowed one from the cattle people, who'd heard it from a tribe on the far side of Zabardu.

'Bambomiyi', they called her, or 'Fathermother'.

When she saw the boy's face, however, the Broken Witch stopped so hard that her bare feet launched a little spray of sand.

"Bambomiyi," Togo said again, even though he could see her.

The Broken Witch regarded Togo, who was a tall boy whose long limbs appeared to go all over the place when he walked. Most of the villagers had a slight upturn at their outer eyes, giving them a look that was slightly ferocious in most cases and very ferocious in the Broken Witch's. Togo, however, had huge, round eyes that made him look permanently surprised and very innocent. This look would make him a problem with the girls when he was older, but currently appearance and reality were conjoined.

The Broken Witch saw that Togo was not carrying a water pouch, and from his panicked expression had probably rushed here without preparing. Like all the village males, his wrap covered his lower body only, which was fine within the confines of the village but less wise out by the wreck. They were now on the cusp of the burning time when the sun approached its height and bore down on the desert like a hot metal sheet.

"Togo," the Broken Witch said.

Her speaking voice was very soft and very low. Her screaming voice was high and piercing, almost like a weapon. She had great range, did the Broken Witch.

"Bambomiyi, please!" Togo said, his thin chest heaving and sweat making his shoulders glitter. "You must come, you must come now!"

"Tell me what the matter is, Togo," the Broken Witch said.

It was always miraculous to her when she spoke to children she had delivered. Here was this fine and unique boy speaking to her and yet when she had first seen him he had been a tiny grey thing approaching a breach birth, necessitating use of the Broken Witch's stonesung knife, a tool that never required sharpening even when her father had used it and was so sharp it needed a stone sheath. Yet the knife was a clumsy thing compared to what the Broken Witch had used before, when her living armour had grown weapons that could cut and heal with equal efficiency, cauterising wounds and sealing them without a scar. The Broken Witch had opened Togo's mother and pulled Togo forth, then had to use the brute violence of sutures and the pincers of head ants the Broken Witch bred and decapitated for the purpose. The scar on Togo's mother was not that bad now, but still felt like an accusation every time the Broken Witch saw it.

"No, no, Bambomiyi – I must bring you!"

"It is the burning time, Togo."

"I don't care!"

"I do."

The Broken Witch gestured at the wreck.

"Come inside."

Togo drew back.

"You told us it was possessed by demons," he said.

"I made that up," the Broken Witch said. "I don't like to be bothered when I'm in one of my moods, or even when I'm not."

Togo stared up at the wreck.

Even the Broken Witch had no idea what the wreck had been. She knew it was old, possibly from the time of the Daxu, when those other-worldly beings had walked among the peoples of the earth, found them beautiful and made love with them, creating a whole new race of whom the Broken Witch was a shattered descendent. The Daxu were long gone though, and their time had ended badly. The Broken Witch was sure the wreck was part of a vehicle, but whether it travelled across the dunes, beneath the sand or flew as the Broken Witch had done on her woodwing was not obvious from the design.

The wreck was tall, thin and roughly pyramidal, although its top was an eerie, gnarled spire that ended in a long point like a thick-bodied spear aimed at the sky. The entire structure was made of a very dark wood, stark against the soft gold of the sand. The wood did not burn, could not be cut and never bleached the way other wood did. There was something like a door, which would have taken at least five large men to yank open, although the Broken Witch lifted it with ease. The doorway could accommodate a figure much larger than anyone in the village, or even the cattle tribe, who rarely grew to less than six and a half feet (much to the Broken Witch's delight). Whatever the wreck had been, it was woodsung, clear from the size and lack of any joins.

There were few trees in this part of Zabardu; the desert didn't favour them. The only one the Broken Witch knew of was the baduba tree in the village, which absorbed the people's bodily wastes. Other wood products were traded for with the passing tribes as they wound their patient way through the great country.

The wreck, then, was from elsewhere. Even the monsters the Broken Witch had fought in the north possessed nothing like it. Equally perplexing was the lack of a Kani Path in the vicinity. The Daxu had drawn together the natural energies of the earth, enhanced and then woven them into a net of power that crisscrossed the world. They and their descendants drew the force they called the Way from this pattern, a power the Broken Witch could no longer engage.

The source of the village's prosperity was its closeness to a Kani Path crossroads, but there was nothing closer. Daxu vehicles only worked along Kani Paths, so what was the wreck doing here? The Broken Witch imagined the sort of cataclysm that could have hurled this great object across the desert and shuddered. All of it felt familiar in a way she could not define, as if Togo's appearance had triggered something that made her view the wreck in a new, disturbing fashion.

Togo was still staring at the wreck, even though the Broken Witch was holding the door open. The Broken Witch cleared her throat. Togo snapped out of his trance and looked at her.

"Please, Bambomiyi," Togo said.

"Is someone dying, Togo?"

The Broken Witch was quite sure nobody was dying but Togo's reaction was still a surprise.

"Not… exactly," Togo said.

Togo's response had an unexpected subtlety. Whatever the problem was, it was new.

"Now then, Togo," the Broken Witch said. "I will come with you, but first you must drink and take my spare wrap for your head."

"Why?"

"Because we are in the burning time. If you do not do as I ask, then you will fall down, and I will have to carry you."

"But you are so strong, Bambomiyi."

"Yes but carrying you will dishevel the wrap I am wearing."

"I understand," Togo said.

"You do? Really?"

Togo looked to his left. The Broken Witch's eyes narrowed. Togo swallowed.

"I will come inside, Bambomiyi," Togo said.

The Broken Witch could tell from the set of the boy's shoulders that he was tense and unhappy. As he walked past into the wreck, his mournful eyes were even wider than usual.

The wreck's interior was like a large, wooden tent. Cracks and openings let in beams of dazzling light, but it was still unusually cool. There was no floor; the desert continued its march through the wreck and out of the other side. There were odd protrusions whose purpose was inexplicable and a few structures that looked like shelves. As without, there was a sense of inhuman scale about everything.

The Broken Witch disliked possessions and had very few. Her only other garment was the spare wrap she pulled from a boxy outcrop four feet off the warm sandy floor and threw to Togo, who caught it one-handed with the easy reflex of youth. The Broken Witch was distracted by discovery of the gugga ball in the same box and so pretended not to see Togo sniff the garment, twitch in surprise at how nice it smelled and then sniff it again, more deeply this time. There was a sleeping sheet the Broken Witch kept for guests, preferring to sleep naked on one of the shelves; the stonesung knife in its smooth rock sheath in pride of place in an alcove on a strut in the centre of the space, and an arrangement of ceramic pots containing various resins. Some of these substances were healing unguents, although the Broken Witch kept most of her medicinal gear hidden around the village where it was most useful. Others were scents she had either accumulated or devised to enhance her own sweet aroma. She pulled one out now and spread a layer of the cool, delicious paste beneath her arms as Togo put the wrap over his head and shoulders to protect them.

The Broken Witch burrowed into the sand and pulled out a large, stoppered stone jug. She pulled the stopper out, lifted her chin at Togo so he tilted his head back and poured water down the boy's throat. From the big, eager gulps, it was clear how thirsty he was; it was some time before he signalled to the Broken Witch to stop, by which time the jug was half empty. The Broken Witch regarded Togo and took a long drink herself. She stoppered the jar, buried it and, from the sand beside it pulled another, this one smaller. She opened it and showed Togo. Inside were six large soft-shelled crustaceans, each of which moved very sluggishly.

"Sand crabs!" said Togo, his mission momentarily forgotten.

"The very same," the Broken Witch said. "What is more, they have drunk the Tears of the Desert and are ready for us."

Togo and the Broken Witch touched each of the crabs in turn to thank them, then ate three each. The creatures were strong and usually fast, their rich flavour a celebration of animal power.

When Togo and the Broken Witch were done, she threw the jar across the space where it clinked against a pile of similar debris. She bade Togo sit by the column with the stonesung knife and knelt opposite him, her slender legs folded prettily beside her. She was sure that Togo would marry someone who looked like her, although probably someone without a Black Lion.

"Tell me then, my friend," the Broken Witch said.

Togo perked up at this adult address, instinctively becoming more formal and accurate.

"There is something in the village," Togo said.

The Broken Witch waited for more, but Togo said nothing, as if he expected the Broken Witch to simply understand.

"What is it?" the Broken Witch said.

Togo swallowed. Before, he had merely been embarrassed and awkward. Now he was scared. He went to speak again but no words came. He pressed his lips together and looked the Broken Witch in the eye. For a time, it seemed as if he was trying to convey something to the Broken Witch by thought alone, but even at the height of her powers the Broken Witch had been unable to pull that trick off. She waited patiently. Togo shook his head and looked much more confused than a nine-year-old boy ever should.

"It's that," Togo said.

The Broken Witch frowned.

"Can you not explain?" she said.

Togo shook his head.

"It is as I just showed you," he said.

"A wordless… dread?" the Broken Witch said.

Togo jerked back, huge-eyed, and pointed at the Broken Witch. The Broken Witch saw that Togo's dark skin was grey with fear and that he was rigid.

"D-dread," Togo said. "That is what it is."

"Dread in the village," the Broken Witch said.

Togo nodded.

"Can you explain it?" he said.

"Not sure," the Broken Witch said. "How does it show itself?"

"It does not."

"How, then, do you know it is there?"

Togo gulped.

"Half the village is empty and everyone who lives and works on that side has come over to the other," he said. "It is as if a straight line has been drawn across the centre, and everything beyond is horror."

The Broken Witch smoothed a patch of sand between them and draw a half-circle in it.

"Let us say this is the village," the Broken Witch said, pointing at the half-circle. "Where does the line cross?"

Togo sat and stared at the shape in the sand. Even its representation scared him; when he reached for it his hand shook. Breathing deeply, he drew his finger across the centre of the half-circle, bisecting it into two quarter circles. The Broken Witch pressed a dent in the sand within the quarter-circle segment nearest Togo.

"This is the Widow Ndugu's hut," the Broken Witch said, indicating the dent. "Is the dread within that half of the village or the other half?"

"The other half."

"You are sure of that?"

"Yes, Bambomiyi."

The Broken Witch settled back with a sigh of relief.

"It is in the south of the village, then," she said.

"Why does that matter?" Togo said.

"I feared that if the dread was in the north of the village then the war might have reached us in some fashion, for the war is in the north of Zabardu, and – and..."

The Broken Witch's gaze drifted, and she shook, as if in an icy draft. Togo watched. Like the other villagers, he was used to this sort of thing.

The Broken Witch pressed her hands to her face, slowly feeling the contours of it as if making sure everything was still there. Dramatic arched brows: yes; high cheekbones: yes; broad but delicate nose: yes; generous abundance of lips: yes; bit of a gap between large, white front teeth: yes; firm, discrete but also somehow lethal chin: very much so. She took her hands away and stared at the design on the floor.

"That is good, then," she said.

The Broken Witch stood and with her bare foot smoothed away the design. She patted sand from her bottom and looked down at Togo.

"Are you ready?"

"I am, but... Bambomiyi, there is something else. One of the villagers is trapped in the far south of the village."

"Trapped in the dread?"

"Yes. We cannot reach them, and they cannot get across."

"Could they not simply run through –?"

"No!"

Togo was on his feet, almost without seeming to move. He shook his head as if to clear it.

"Forgive my rudeness, Bambomiyi. But no, they cannot. It is hard to explain unless you have been there and felt it for yourself."

"Who is this unfortunate?"

Togo spoke a name, but for some reason the Broken Witch did not hear it. She knew that Togo had said something, but the sound existed without meaning. The Broken Witch was resigned to these lapses; she nodded to acknowledge that she had heard something, even though she had not understood it. Togo frowned, but said nothing more.

The Broken Witch thought for a moment, then filled the pockets of her wrap with pinches of ointment and powder. She dug transparent cream from a final jar and smoothed some across Togo's face, shoulders and arms.

"To keep the worst of the burning time from you."

Togo screwed up his nose.

"Do not struggle, young man," the Broken Witch said. "You will thank me when you are older. Do you know my age?"

"Thirty-nine years and four months, Bambomiyi."

The Broken Witch drew back.

"Who told you that?"

"You did, Bambomiyi."

The Broken Witch considered.

"When was this?" she said.

"Last week," Togo said.

"Was I in my right mind?"

"Most definitely not, Bambomiyi."

"Hm. Well, we shall leave it at that then, other than to say one does not look this good at my age by unguarded exposure to the burning time."

The Broken Witch rubbed the gel onto her own face and

arms and then smoothed it into her hair, making it shine even more. The Broken Witch took the stonesung knife from its alcove in the column, pulled the end of the wrap free, tied the knife into it so the weight was evenly distributed, and re-tucked the end of the wrap. Finally, she dug the water jug up again and put it under one arm.

"We can finish this on the journey," she said. "I need to fill it up at the village anyway."

Togo stared at the Broken Witch. He said the name of the trapped person again, and again the Broken Witch did not comprehend it. She smiled to reassure Togo.

"We can go now, Togo," the Broken Witch said.

She hoisted the door open and followed the boy out.

The Burning Time

The burning time was well underway when Togo and the Broken Witch set off. Although they walked at a measured pace, each inhaled breath felt like it was gently cooking their lungs and their tough soles barely weathered the heat coming off the desert.

The air seethed around them like an echo of the great dunes that rippled into the bright horizon. The embrace of tall heat was inspiring and exhausting, carrying the smell of a continent's worth of geology, ground and mixed until it was spicy.

The Broken Witch always felt calm in the desert. She knew her limits, for all that she regularly exceeded them. She had faith in Togo too, who had been wise enough to let her look after him. They would make good time and arrive safely, despite the incalculable volume and shifting distance around them.

And… was there a hint of excitement in the Broken Witch's step?

Togo was happier now he had the Broken Witch with him. It was just as well. The desert was unforgiving at the best of times and seemed to take particular pride in sucking the essence from weepy hysteria, as the Broken Witch knew from bitter experience.

The wreck was some way behind them now, out of sight behind the dunes, whose long, sharpened crests were so exquisitely wrought that a fine sandy mist occasionally soared into the sky in the hot light breeze, as if the dune tips were cutting through the air and leaving stone shavings in their wake. Togo and the Broken Witch stepped lightly across the heated surface, sand abrading their feet as they sank into the warm, granular depths.

The village drew them, its attraction unmistakable across the vacant beauty of the landscape. It was a human thing, this pull towards home. Perhaps it was the feel of the sun, perhaps the muscle memory of so many journeys back and forth, or perhaps it was the yearning for an anchor in a mobile land: a respite from its overwhelming glory.

They reached the Kani Path that crossed the desert, a path not often used these days. There was evidence of travel though, in the compacted sand and the worn remains of discarded crockery.

The Broken Witch tried to ignore a persistent, residual anticipation. The invisible Kani Path was sunk deep into the earth and reached high into the sky: a corridor of complex, living power that linked with, conveyed and nourished the dizzying world pattern the Daxu had left behind. As a Daxu Cross, the Broken Witch had once been able to channel and manipulate the Way no matter where she was, but its music was always strongest along the Paths.

The Broken Witch felt nothing, however; it was just

another patch of desert. She took a series of short, sniffing breaths, touched her hair and looked at Togo.

"Good boy," she said.

He turned to her, confused and then stared at his feet.

They went on and soon the village became visible on the horizon. At first it was a difference in colour: a strip of white against the implacable gold of the desert, like a mirage. Then the sand began to coarsen, turning to gravel and finally to rock.

The desert had many faces and the village was on the border between two of them. The habitation was like a harbour in the fertile, rocky plains, facing a deep, mysterious ocean of sand. They reached the crossing of one Kani Path and another, the latter a more obvious route marked at the edges with stones and with a few travellers on it, their goods lifted by engagements with the Way that enabled heavy items to be pulled along like balloons.

One was a cattle tribesman, who the Broken Witch remembered curing of venereal disease last year. At the time, it had frustrated her that she couldn't make love with him; but the village had to be protected. The cattle tribe were particularly susceptible to this sort of infection as they ranged over the whole of Zabardu, plus they were beautiful.

This fellow had a long, rangy body and gleaming skin that was a shade darker than even the Broken Witch's. The cattle man enjoyed a brutal, pouty masculinity, and a breadth of shoulder and narrowness of waist that distracted the Broken Witch from her misery at the silence of the Kani Paths, and indeed from her present mission until Togo pulled his charge none too gently by the finger.

The Broken Witch tutted, then turned and watched the cattle man pass. He had one of his tribe's lovely, long-horned white cows with him: a dreamy-looking animal with something of a swagger, sustained by a big skin of water and a tight-packed grass bundle whose undersides hung two feet above her. She pulled them along on a thin stonesung disc that was bound about with rope, and which drifted in the air of the Kani Path as if both stone and burdens weighed nothing.

The cattle man looked at the Broken Witch, who lowered her sleek head, let her eyes go slightly out of focus and her lips part to reveal the little gap in her teeth. The cattle man jutted his blocky chin at her in the tribe's artless but practical version of a greeting. He passed close enough for the Broken Witch to get his scent. No infection. Good.

"Next time," the Broken Witch mouthed at the cattle man.

The cattle man grunted and walked on, but the Broken Witch noticed that his broad, muscle-padded chest was rising and falling faster than it had before. Ha.

"Bambomiyi!"

"Yes, yes Togo, do calm down."

"No, it's just… er… That," Togo said and pointed.

The village was close enough that the rise of its back wall was visible like a white mound. In front of the broad, open mouth of the settlement stood twenty villagers. They didn't look pleased to see the Broken Witch, and some were carrying clubs.

"Eh?" the Broken Witch said.

One of the villagers, a man of about thirty, stepped forward and pointed at the Broken Witch.

"You have done this!" he shouted.

The Broken Witch looked at Togo, whose blank face and slack jaw made it clear he had no idea what was going on. The Broken Witch turned back to her accuser.

"Done what?" the Broken Witch said.

"Brought this horror on us!"

The Broken Witch felt a sudden ache in her gut. Had she been mistaken about the venereal disease? Was her well-honed sense for illness in decline along with everything else?

"He means the dread," Togo whispered.

"I don't even know about the dread!" the Broken Witch screamed at the man.

Everyone jumped, even Togo. The Broken Witch's mood swings were well-known yet also unexpected, even to her. The man swallowed but didn't move. He tightened his grip on the club, which the Broken Witch noticed was part of a paddle used to skim the algae ponds. The others carried the same implements. They were mostly men, plus the few women immune to the Broken Witch's charms, which the Broken Witch put down to envy.

She knew the man in front. He was not immune to the Broken Witch's charms and had availed himself of them on many occasions, to their mutual delight. The Broken Witch suspected she had been his first lover, after delirious ramblings to that effect as she soothed his brow during a bout of tinge fever. He denied it later and she had attempted to get the truth by withholding favours. He had followed her out to the wreck with a jug of milk liquor and after a few pints the Broken Witch quickly forgot her reticence.

She didn't recognise him today, though.

"You are not natural!" shouted the man, who the Broken

Witch remembered was called Adebinte.

The Broken Witch sighed. Soon, someone would refer to her as 'it'.

"You found me natural enough before, Adebinte," she said.

"Liar!" Adebinte shouted.

"But Adebinte," one of the women said, "you told us that —"

"Shush, please," Adebinte said, his voice strained.

"We must get past," Togo said, but nobody listened.

"If we kill her —" Adebinte said.

"Kill it you mean," another man said.

The Broken Witch sighed again.

Adebinte glared at the man, although the Broken Witch knew the source of Adebinte's anger was the interruption, not the sentiment.

"If we kill it then the dread will be lifted," Adebinte finished.

"How do you work that out?" the Broken Witch said.

"It is some evil you brought back from the war," Adebinte said.

"The war," said the other man.

"The war I returned from fourteen years ago?" the Broken Witch said.

"You were much changed," Adebinte said.

"War does that," the Broken Witch said, "not that you'd know, Adebinte."

Adebinte flushed.

"Besides," the Broken Witch continued, "if the war was the source of the dread and me its conveyance, would it not have appeared sooner?"

"Not necessarily," Adebinte said and the others murmured their approval.

The Broken Witch could feel one of her moods coming on. She struggled against it, but when she spoke her voice was flat.

"And when I am battered to pieces, who will deliver your children and cure your sick?" the Broken Witch said.

"The Widow Ndugu," Adebinte said.

"The Widow Ndugu is nowhere near as good as me," the Broken Witch said.

"We will find a way," Adebinte said.

The Broken Witch waited for him to elaborate but he didn't, which put an unexpected end to the debate.

"We must get past, Bambomiyi," Togo said.

The Broken Witch looked at the boy, who had tears in his eyes.

"They are too many," the Broken Witch said.

"But you are so strong," Togo said.

"Not that strong."

"The women are smaller."

"Women are fast and cunning and better with weapons than they pretend," the Broken Witch said.

"Please," the boy said. "These do not speak for all."

The Broken Witch went to suggest the 'all' come forth from the village and sort this foolery out but stopped. It wasn't Togo's fault.

"For you then, Togo my friend," the Broken Witch said.

Togo's smile gave her such strength she forgot the silent Kani Paths and her vanished power. She dropped the empty water jug, turned again to Adebinte and reached for the stonesung knife.

There was a scream from the village!

Everybody went still. The Broken Witch's hand was motionless before the stonesung knife in her wrap; Togo's eyes were huge with fear and Adebinte had the panicked look of one who has assumed power, then realised he has no idea what to do with it.

More people ran from the village, dark figures against the pale rock. At the front was the Headmun, only a year into his role and still at the bossy stage rather than the useful one. He was twenty-five and more heavy-set than Adebinte, although the latter was taller.

"Bambomiyi!" the Headmun shouted. "Why do you dally here?"

"I am not dallying!" the Broken Witch screamed.

"Oh dear," Togo said.

With effort, the Broken Witch got herself under control and flapped a hand at Adebinte.

"These rabbits obstruct me," the Broken Witch said. "If it was that important, perhaps you could have met me yourself."

Adebinte pointed at the Broken Witch.

"She has brought the dread upon us," Adebinte said.

"*It*," the other man said.

"Shut your mouth," Adebinte told him.

The Headmun, whose youth meant he was less worn down by rocklike stupidity than the Broken Witch, stared at Adebinte. Adebinte sneered down at the Headmun, who then punched Adebinte in the face. Adebinte fell down and stayed there. Twenty more villagers had run out with the Headmun and these joined the Headmun in glaring at Adebinte's followers as their leader commenced an involuntary doze. Adebinte's followers backed away.

"Yes!" one of them shouted for some reason and then they all ran off.

The Headmun rushed over to the Broken Witch.

"I am sorry, Bambomiyi," the Headmun said. "I did not know. Please come."

The Broken Witch nodded and went to step forward but before she could move the Headmun took her hand, gripped it tight and began to sprint back towards the village. The Broken Witch ran alongside the Headman with Togo and the other villagers fanning out either side, keeping pace. The Broken Witch glanced around as she ran. Everyone looked terrified.

Presently, they reached the village entrance, where the opening of its C-shape faced the desert. The tips of the C were close to the ground but rose sharply as they curved around the back of the village, with the great baduba tree nestling against the far wall like a slow-shattering emerald in the morning sun. The C was semi-circular in cross-section with the flat side down, creating a streamlined barrier against invasion and sandstorms, which usually came from the west.

The wall and the space beneath it formed a complex of stonesung caves, designed so that air and heat moved through them at optimum levels. In some areas the rock was transparent, allowing in the sunlight but modifying the heat so the algae that kept the drinking water clean and provided the village's staple foodstuff could flourish.

There were deep cold stores under there, close to the aquifer that irrigated the area. The same water fed a nearby oasis frequented by wild animals, as well as hot-stone chambers, steams and ovens. There were homes and crèches and retreats, places of study and workshops.

The Broken Witch's father had occupied one of the latter, where he had stone-sung products for trade and village use. Now that he was dead, his workshop was used by the man who lay crumpled in the open space at the heart of the village, where the circular huts thinned out.

The Broken Witch stepped towards the fallen man but the Headmun grabbed her from behind.

"No Bambomiyi!"

The Broken Witch disliked this kind of manhandling and wriggled free. The Headmun stepped back and pointed to the ground, where a straight line drawn in charcoal bisected the C-shape of the village, dividing it neatly in two. The line went all the way to the opening in the modesty wall around the baduba tree. The straight marking became jerky here and there and was part-scrubbed out in places, as if the person drawing it had suffered seizures.

"Do not cross the line, Bambomiyi," the Headmun said. He hesitated and then went on: "At least, not yet."

The Broken Witch pointed at the area containing the fallen man.

"That is where the dread is," she said.

The Headmun nodded and spoke a couple of words, which the Broken Witch again failed to comprehend.

"She does not hear the name," Togo said to the Headmun.

The Broken Witch walked along the dividing line between the empty part of the village and the other, which was beginning to fill as people came up from the caves and out of their huts to see what was happening. She heard panicked discussions behind her but ignored them as she peered through the brightness at the figure on the ground.

Turning, she saw a crying woman nearby. The Broken Witch knew she liked the woman; that the woman was important to her somehow. If only she could remember the woman's name! She crossed to the woman and took her hands.

"Bambomiyi," the woman said. "Please save her."

"Her?"

The Broken Witch turned to the fallen figure. There was no doubt it was a man.

"He tried to save her by going over the wall, but he fell."

The Broken Witch gasped. The wall's curve and smoothness made it impossible to scale. She could well imagine the desperation that drove someone to such a hopeless act.

The woman stepped up to the Broken Witch and stroked her face. The Broken Witch turned to the woman again.

"You know us," the woman said. "You love us."

The Broken Witch nodded. It seemed likely. The woman was finely made, with the sort of bushy hair the Broken Witch dreamed of, gracefully curved hips and gentle eyes. The pretty woman pointed at the fallen man.

"You call him the Stonesinger, and I am his wife."

The Broken Witch staggered back, shaking violently, as if Adebinte and his friends were hitting her with their clubs.

The Stonesinger.

Of course.

Somehow, she was kneeling. Her hands shook and her eyes refused to focus. She felt as though she was lying down, although she knew she was upright. The Stonesinger's wife knelt beside her and put an arm around her shoulders.

"It is Precious Child who is trapped on the far side of the village," the Stonesinger's wife said.

Delicacy

Six years previously, the Stonesinger and his wife had approached the Broken Witch and told her they yearned for a child. They had been married for eight years and despite coupling twice a day had thus far not conceived. Could the Broken Witch help?

The Broken Witch had glared at them. She resented her father's workshop being used by the Stonesinger, even though the Stonesinger had been her father's apprentice, was a gifted artisan whose produce benefited the village, and whose occupation of the workshop was the express desire of the Broken Witch's father upon his death. The Broken Witch knew full well she was being unreasonable, but she was a witch and she was broken and being unreasonable was entirely her prerogative.

The Stonesinger and his wife apologised to the Broken Witch for bothering her and withdrew. Immediately, the Broken Witch felt wretched and horrible. She ran after the couple and stopped them.

"I miss my father," the Broken Witch said.

"So do we," the Stonesinger said.

The Broken Witch nodded.

"It is hard for me," the Broken Witch went on, "to know that you are in his workshop and he is not. Even though I am glad you are there, that my father's apprentice took over his craft and kept it alive."

The Stonesinger's wife touched the Broken Witch on the arm. It was a nice tickling sensation. The Broken Witch swallowed.

"It is, I think, why I can never remember your names," the Broken Witch said. "It is not disrespect. It is that you remind me my father is dead."

She closed her eyes and an old, usually controlled sense of self-loathing bubbled up. She breathed deeply; the hatred seemed to go. She looked at the Stonesinger and his wife again.

"Forgive my rudeness," the Broken Witch said. "Of course I will help you, if I can."

The Stonesinger smiled. He was not as pretty as his wife, but there was a happiness about him that was more satisfying than a pleasing surface. More beguiling still was that love between man and wife, as if they were two parts of the same person. Each of them took one of the Broken Witch's hands and led her across the busy village to an opening in the stone wall.

They descended a flight of steps that zig-zagged back on themselves until the three people were walking through a series of linked tunnels under the village. Light entered through discreet openings and reflected off pale rock, while pressure changes created by variations in temperature and moisture content kept the air lively and fresh.

The Stonesinger went first, his hand lightly entwined with the Broken Witch's. After the Broken Witch came the Stonesinger's wife. Her grip was tight with the palms noticeably dryer than those of the Broken Witch, who was getting nervous as she tried to recall if she had ever created fertility where there had been none before.

When she had contemplated making her own womb, it had been an essentially simple proposition to enable an aspect of herself that was implicitly already present. Even that had taken considerable research, flying the Kani Paths across Zabardu on her woodwing to seek the Realms of Knowing. And in the end, she had not done it; enjoying the power of being able to make one choice, only to make another.

This was different. She was not even sure if fertility was the problem; she would need to check. They were walking fast, which meant that the Broken Witch could not get a good scent, particularly down here in the caves where the air was boisterous with movement and other smells: cooking, sleeping, farming; all the various crafts of the village and the Way.

They arrived at the workshop and the Broken Witch looked around. With a jolt, she realised she had not been here since her return from the war.

There were different grades of stonesinger. The Daxu had enjoyed supreme command of the element; it was they who had formed the village: a marvel of structural, environmental and biological engineering whose construction was now beyond the ability of even their most gifted descendants. No aspect of the village required mechanical input other than the natural movement of air and heat over the desert, the pressure of stone, and the physical processes of its inhabitants.

Human stonesingers ranged from those who cracked underground rock for extraction or made roads, those who reformed blocks, so they looked like this leader or that, and those who worked at a more refined scale as artisans. The Stonesinger and the Broken Witch's father were the latter.

The workshop was a hemispherical space on the Daxu scale with a stone bench that jutted out all around the circular wall. There was a light well, a flue for the rare occasions there were dust or chippings and two more chimneys for supply and extract ventilation. A pool of cold water bubbled up in a waist-high bowl atop a column in the centre of the room.

Dozens of models and works in progress were stacked neatly under the bench, along with completed dig-blades, knives, algae setters, jugs, harness fastenings, bench footings and lifting discs. Uncannily detailed little sculptures depicted people from visiting tribes, animals, and even a miniature of the village itself. A gallery of gems in a large case under a clear rock sheet flashed as the Broken Witch walked into the workshop. She paused to look at the jewellery, made from a hundred different stones. Some were as large as a thumb; others were hints of coloured light that glittered in the sun shining through openings in the roof.

The Broken Witch did not begrudge the Stonesinger his connection to the Way. The Stonesinger's ability lay in rearranging matrices at the heart of rock. He would find the structure's endless possibilities and hone them down to one with a mathematical language that felt like music.

Despite her father's craft, the Broken Witch had no ability with stone. Her material was subtler and more terrifying: the supremely delicate yet infinitely malleable frequencies of the flesh. Her lost power was thus orders of magnitude greater than the Stonesinger's, and the music she had heard would have deafened him or been perceived as silence.

The Broken Witch followed the Stonesinger into the dwelling behind the workshop, only to stop short when she saw it was almost unchanged. The same low, rare wood table sat in the alcove under the skylight with the same cushioned benches either side of it, although the table now supported a pot of red and orange desert blooms. The sleeping alcove was screened by the same dark blue curtain with the intricate, interwoven design that looked like everything and nothing at the same time. The same elegant, simple and yet dauntingly complex Daxu markings adorned the left-hand wall; markings that might have been instruction, language or decoration – no one could agree which. Home, then, and yet not.

The Stonesinger turned and smiled again. It was impossible to feel awkward around him. His wife still held the Broken Witch's hand, the lovely woman's cool, dry grip both a welcome and a comfort. The Stonesinger gestured to the thick, round mat on the floor, whose dune-like wavy pattern and deep, sandy colour were more familiar, the mat being one of the village's more popular products. The Broken Witch stared at the mat. Unlike other parts of the home, she could not remember if the mat had been her father's. On reflection, she thought not. Her father was not given to luxuries.

The Stonesinger's wife sat and gently pulled the Broken Witch down beside her. The Stonesinger fetched a jug that from its similarity in shape to those in the workshop was clearly his own design, and poured clear fluid into three cups. He gave one to the Broken Witch, one to his wife and then sat beside them on the mat, placing the jug nearby.

Each of them wrapped their fingers around the cup and

stared for a moment into the depths. They raised their eyes and looked at each other in turn. Then they drank.

The Broken Witch was surprised to find the fluid was milk liqueur, and a well-refined volume at that. She stopped herself taking more than a medium sip and placed the cup down.

"This thing you ask," she said. "There is a process we must undertake before we begin anything else."

"We understand," the Stonesinger's wife said.

"You should know that I may not be able to help you."

"We are grateful that you will try, Bambomiyi," the Stonesinger said.

The Broken Witch nodded. She looked at the cup again; tried to ignore it.

"We must first see if you are both fertile," the Broken Witch said.

The couple nodded, their eyes anxious. The Broken Witch nodded too, then fixed her eyes on the Stonesinger's wife.

"It is easier with the woman, so…"

"Of course," the Stonesinger's wife said.

For a moment, nobody moved.

"Um, what do you want me to do, Bambomiyi?"

"Oh! Er, just stand for me please."

Gracefully, the woman got up.

"Here?"

"Yes, thank you."

"What do you do, exactly?" the woman asked.

"Most of the time I use smell. Sometimes taste and touch also."

"I see," the woman said.

"Listen," the Broken Witch said, "you both know me, or know of me."

"Yes," the Stonesinger said.

"I am a person of great passions," the Broken Witch said.

"You could put it that way," the Stonesinger said.

"Hm," the Broken Witch said. "But you must understand that although you are both beautiful I – I… You can trust that I do this, today, now, for your good and not my own, er, interests. And because you asked me to, knowing that I am, after all, me –"

"Bambomiyi," the Stonesinger's wife said.

"Yes?"

"Get on with it."

The Broken Witch had done so and found that the Stonesinger had no seed. There seemed little to be done. Even at the height of her powers, the Broken Witch could not create life where none existed; she suspected such a feat had even been beyond the Daxu. Saddened, she had left them and returned to the wreck in the desert. However, the following day, the Stonesinger and his wife had invited the Broken Witch to dinner.

Over a rich beef stew, several cups of sweet milk liqueur and a smoke pot of transformational herbs the Stonesinger had invited the Broken Witch to impregnate his wife.

The Stonesinger had foundling brothers he loved as deeply as he did those of his own blood and yearned for a child as much as his wife did. The Broken Witch had no children, not because she did not love them but because she felt that a person who couldn't remember her own name might not be a child's best start in life. So, she had agreed, and the three had gone to bed together, and nine months later the Broken Witch delivered Precious Child.

Into the Dread

The Broken Witch and the Stonesinger's Wife faced the dread that occupied half the village. The Broken Witch grunted and was off before anyone could stop her, across the line in the ground and –

She woke up, curled on the rocky floor of the village, back beside the Stonesinger's wife. The Stonesinger was still in the same position and Precious Child was nowhere to be seen. It appeared to be raining, until the Broken Witch realised that the Stonesinger's wife was crying and the tears were falling on the Broken Witch's face.

The Broken Witch tried to speak but could not. She knew that a person is made of innumerable tiny elements, all carefully arranged. A moment in the dread felt like a disruption of that intimate pattern, like exposure to intense heat. The dread wasn't hot, however. It was not cold either.

It was not really anything.

The Broken Witch groaned. Sensation came back and with it shame. How foolish she had been to rush in like that, as if she was still powerful rather than broken.

What a fool. What a freak. What a useless object.

Whose voice was saying such cruel things? It sounded like her own. But why?

The Broken Witch slumped against the ground. She felt as if she had become liquid. Aware of soreness down one side and an ache in her right ankle, she looked across the ground and saw rope around her right foot.

On the Broken Witch's other side squatted the Widow Ndugu. Although the Widow's face was inexpressive as usual, she was out of breath. The Broken Witch had a grim sense that she would be feeling much worse if the Widow Ndugu had not moved so fast.

Looking down between the Widow Ndugu and the Stonesinger's wife was the Headmun. The Broken Witch could sense the other villagers gathered around; the comforting presence of many people, waiting.

They were wrong to trust her, to expect anything. It was time they knew.

The Broken Witch found her voice.

"I am broken, Headmun. I am a broken witch, for my power is gone."

"Yes, yes, we know all that," the Headmun said.

"Uh?"

"We know and we love you still. That is the only weapon I can give you against this enemy. We love you. All of us. Remember that."

"Adebinte –?"

"Adebinte is a beetle of the eighth water who loves you and will not admit it, because he is filled with terror."

"Of my beauty?"

"No, Bambomiyi, of the dread."

"Oh, yes."

The Broken Witch looked at the Stonesinger's wife.

"When your husband fell, did he hit his head?"

"I do not know," the Stonesinger's wife said. "It happened too fast."

"What did you hear?" the Broken Witch said.

"The horrible snap of his wound."

"Did he cry out after that?"

"No," the Widow Ndugu said.

With effort, the Broken Witch raised her head, so she was looking at the Stonesinger.

"It may be that he is senseless, and that he does not feel the dread because he is asleep," the Broken Witch said. "I will get him first and tend to him, and then I will go for Precious Child."

"But Bambomiyi –!"

The Broken Witch used all her strength to get up and stood, swaying. The Stonesinger's wife looked at the Broken Witch with wide and desperate eyes. The Broken Witch turned away from her and gazed across the dread.

"I make the Choice," the Broken Witch said. "I choose who is healed and when and how, and I bear the blame and the responsibility. I absolve you and the Headmun of it – not that you had a say, Arjana."

The Stonesinger's wife gasped.

"You remember my name!" she said.

"Of course I do," the Broken Witch snapped and then realised. "Oh."

They all reflected on this development, and then the Broken Witch reached down and pulled the Stonesinger's wife to her feet.

"Precious Child must have her father and you must have your husband," the Broken Witch said. "He is wounded, and I will tend to him. Precious Child is out of sight, possibly within the caves on the far side of the village. Perhaps the dread does not reach that far, or underground."

"It is not safe there in other ways," the Stonesinger's wife said. "There are the algae ponds –"

"If Precious Child has fallen in there, then it is already too late," the Broken Witch said, her low voice calm. "I think it is unlikely though, because Precious Child is not an idiot."

There were murmurs of agreement. After a moment, the Stonesinger's wife nodded.

"We must think and understand," the Headmun said, "and do it quickly."

Now she was standing, things were coming back to the Broken Witch.

"I can tell you this dread is not of the Way," she said.

"How do you know?" the Headmun said.

"You recall the great thunderstorms that come with the late season rains?" the Broken Witch said. "Imagine a storm far larger that attacks the world."

"That is how it is," somebody said.

"Yes, but this dread storm is *silent*," the Broken Witch said. "There is no music to it. It feels as if you are lying, horribly injured, and life is going on around you and you can hear it but are trapped, at once close by and far away. It is not something I could engage with, even were I not broken."

She felt invigorating relief that the village knew the truth.

"Bambomiyi understands," Togo said from behind the

Headmun.

Togo's words prompted something in the Broken Witch, something about their time in the wreck.

"I need a vehicle," the Broken Witch said, looking at the fallen Stonesinger.

"There is none here," the Headmun said.

"Yes, there is," the Broken Witch said.

She took a few steps and staggered. The Stonesinger's wife and the Widow Ndugu stepped forward and held the Broken Witch up.

"The dread has affected you worse than any of us, Bambomiyi," the Headmun said. "We should reconsider."

"No," the Broken Witch said. "It must be me, for only I have seen its true face. I cannot tell you what it is yet, but…"

She turned and looked across the empty half of the village. The horror of it seemed to inspire her and she stepped away from the two women.

"Headmun," she said, her voice quick and urgent. "We must make the village look as normal as possible, perhaps with people hiding in caves. They will be safely out of the way and it will not look odd."

"Odd to whom, Bambomiyi?" Togo said.

"Odd to my friend," the Broken Witch said, undoing the rope around her ankle and picking it up.

She began to walk through the villagers, still unsteady and full of a strange, deep nausea. The people around her moved, but everything appeared too slow, even her steps. She started to run in the late morning heat; her usual terrific pace altered so she appeared to topple forward with every step.

Soon the Broken Witch was out of the village and along

the Kani Path, where she dropped the rope. She used her great strength to focus her movement, so she did not look as awkward as she felt, stretching her legs carefully as she ran, feeling her hair stream out behind her.

The cattle man and his cow were a black and white mark in the distance, the stonesung disc bobbing along behind them in the air.

"Hey!" she called.

Even from here, the Broken Witch could see the big man smile at the sight of her. He stopped, turned the cow around and came back towards the Broken Witch. She closed the distance between them, ran up to the cattle man and threw her arms around his neck. His hands moved over her, eased by the slick of sweat on her arms and shoulders. He moved her under the shade of the stonesung disc, where cool air dropped around her.

"I cannot wait," the Broken Witch gasped. "*I cannot.*"

The cattle man moved faster than the Broken Witch expected. He turned her, lifted her and placed her over the back of the cow, up near the head where the animal's legs could take additional weight. The Broken Witch knew this position was a great honour among the cattle tribe. Her hair tumbled down the other side of the cow, dark against its creamy coat as the cattle man lifted the Broken Witch's wrap and pressed himself against the Glory. She allowed him to think he was nearly there, then slipped over the back of the cow so that the animal was between her and her suitor.

She let her desperation show, knowing he would interpret it as desire.

"But…?" the cattle man said.

"Not here, my sweet," the Broken Witch said. "Come back to the village. Quick! I ache for you."

"Here is fine."

"Here is not fine. You will have me and leave me senseless for others to take advantage of."

The cattle man thought for a moment, and then nodded. He tapped the cow across her back in a series of gestures the Broken Witch memorised. The cow began walking back to the village, still between the cattle man and the Broken Witch. The Broken Witch played with her hair, sometimes flicking it back and sometimes stroking it, walking with her chest proudly out. The cattle man tripped a few times, because he was unable to keep his gaze on the Path.

There was a gurgle from the cow's guts, and she kept nosing for the grass pack, but the eager cattle man prompted her along before she could eat.

"You are evil!" someone shouted.

The Broken Witch turned to see Adebinte and his followers run from around the back of the village wall. The cattle man rumbled dangerously. Adebinte's nose was bleeding and he looked as unsteady as the Broken Witch felt.

"Have you come to undo your wicked work?" Adebinte shouted.

The group spread across the entrance to the village, which looked deserted.

"Yes," the Broken Witch replied. "Please help me, Adebinte."

"You would enchant me and make me yours!" Adebinte yelled.

"I have already done that," the Broken Witch said.

"Eh?" the cattle man said.

"Do not worry," the Broken Witch said. "Desire has addled his mind."

"You will make things worse," Adebinte said. "You will cover the whole village in dread."

"Dread?" the cattle man said.

The Broken Witch could sense the cattle man's growing unease. She looked around, saw the Widow Ndugu's rope and picked it up.

Adebinte's followers began to smack their clubs against their palms. The cattle man put his long arm around the Broken Witch's waist.

"I will take you to a safe place," the cattle man said.

He began to draw her away. The Broken Witch resisted, then went quietly. Behind them, Adebinte and his followers jeered. The cattle man tapped his guidance onto the cow, which huffed and turned. Soon they were back on the Kani Path again. When the jeering had quietened, the Broken Witch turned to the cattle man.

"Forgive me, my sweet," the Broken Witch said.

She dropped him with a single blow, then caught him as he fell, lowering him carefully to the ground. She pulled out the stonesung knife, tugged it from its sheath and cut through the rope holding the disc to the cow. The Broken Witch tied the disc with its cooling shade to the limbs of the cattle man so the sun would be off him as he slept. She then jumped up and sliced through the rope that held the tight-packed grass and the water aloft.

The Broken Witch caught the grass, but the water hit the ground. Its container burst and splashed the cow, who set off in the wrong direction. The Broken Witch dropped the grass, ran after the cow and tapped the guide sequence on her back. The cow slowed and the Broken Witch fixed the rope to the animal's long, slender horns. The Broken Witch pulled the cow around until she was facing the village entrance and picked up the grass again.

Adebinte and his followers stared at the Broken Witch, the unconscious cattle man, and the meandering cow with rope on her horns. The Broken Witch staggered as if she was drunk, a common enough sight. It was only when the Broken Witch picked up the heavy grass and hurled it into the dread that Adebinte realised what was happening, but by then it was too late.

The Broken Witch slid onto the cow's back, wound both hands into the rope and spurred the animal forth with a sharp dig in the rump from both feet. The hungry cow chased after the grass through Adebinte and his followers before most of them could get their clubs up. A few blows landed on the Broken Witch; one hit her head and made the world slip.

Then she was through them, into the village and into the dread.

The cow screamed.

It was the sound of a creature who has encountered something unbearably greater than itself and all the cow could do was continue her galloping rush towards the grass.

On the cow's back, the Broken Witch fared little better as the terrible silent storm engulfed her again.

It was a storm of within and without, able to use consciousness as its raw material like a desert storm uses sand. The Broken Witch felt as if she was being whirled in a circle with her feet at the centre, so fast that her mind wanted to fly from her ears. Worse was the ripping conflict between impression and physical reality, as if the nightmare raged through all dimensions. Past, present, future and dream blended and tightened into their most compressed state: a high note that shredded everything but could still be heard.

It was so hard to remember anything. The Broken Witch had kept her plan simple so she would not have it torn from her, but her thoughts were like individual grains of sand blown in all directions. Instead, other memories returned: the mile-high cliffs at the edge of Zabardu, the ocean beyond not of sand but of water; a blue-grey, moving desert, alien and beguiling. And down there in the water was –

No, that was gone; instead she remembered guilt about… about…

She did not want to think about it, not now, as time shook like the desperate breath of a fevered man.

The cow; smell the cow – her bovine scent, the smell of a big beast carrying the absurd weight of her own beautiful fertility, like the stonesung sculpture of a queen. The Broken Witch tried to speak to the cow, to thank her, to apologise for this awful cruelty. But the Broken Witch's voice was a small, hopeless buzz, its pitiful cadence useless in the void.

The Broken Witch had little idea of where they were in relation to the Stonesinger. On one level, vision was possible; this half of the village remained brightly lit under the perfectly ordinary late-morning sun. The nature of the village enabled the ease of heat within its wall, so the sun was never as overpowering or dangerous as it was outside.

However, the dread ripped all utility from these sensations.

Up was down, the sun was black, the cool air boiling. The Broken Witch and the cow could have been falling straight off the earth into the sky and beyond. There was no sense of place, despite the simple sound of galloping hooves and the gasping breath of the woman being carried.

The Broken Witch tried to use her strength, but her body refused to obey. The ropes were helping, and the Broken Witch had mounted the cow in as good a position as she could manage, but if the animal swerved and the Broken Witch fell off, she would either be crushed or stranded. Crushed would be better, by far.

The Broken Witch could feel the dread stripping her down, her sense of self going along with her physicality, despite her Daxu strength.

More unwanted memories now: a battle, far below her, the smell of blood…

A name. What…?

And in the sky –

The Broken Witch beheld a horror within herself to match the engulfing dread and screamed.

For a moment, everything was clear.

She saw she was nearly upon the Stonesinger and leapt off the cow, wrenching the animal about. The cow would not slow and skidded, her legs buckling so that she was almost lying down. The Broken Witch bit through the rope holding her right hand, reached down, gathered up the Stonesinger and pulled him on top of both her and the cow as the cow scrambled back towards the line in the centre of the village. The Stonesinger's broken leg flapped, but the Broken Witch could do nothing except grip him tightly as the cow lunged over the line.

The villagers ran out of their hiding places but ducked back as the cow ran towards them. The Broken Witch bit through the other rope, gripped the Stonesinger and slid off the cow. The Broken Witch grunted as she hit the ground with the Stonesinger on top of her, but the pain was distant, as if it was happening to someone else. The cow kept running and did not stop until her head slammed against the village wall with a dreadful *crack* that snapped off both her horns and killed her at once.

The Broken Witch still held the Stonesinger, who lay senseless upon her. She stroked the back of his head with a trembling hand, the only comfort she could manage, and wept for the cow, her friend's wealth and his status.

Presently, the Stonesinger was lifted off the Broken Witch and she felt the sun. She was unable to move, and the dread washed through her like a dirty, grey liquid. She knew it had marked her and wondered if she would recover enough to find Precious Child.

Voices moved around her like soft wind as shadows crossed her body. Someone knelt and lifted the Broken Witch into a sitting position. The cool, round edge of a cup pressed to her mouth, and lemon water trickled down her throat. She sucked the liquid down, thirstier than if she'd been out in the desert for a day.

Things came into focus. The Broken Witch was supported on one side by the Stonesinger's wife and on the other by Togo. The Stonesinger's wife lifted the cup away.

The Broken Witch looked at her and tried to explain how she wanted to go back for Precious Child but was unsure if it was physically possible for now. What came out was a peculiar croak. The Stonesinger's wife lifted the cup to the Broken Witch's lips again. When the Broken Witch had drunk, she looked around.

The Stonesinger lay on his back nearby, his body cushioned by a mat. The Widow Ndugu had set the Stonesinger's leg straight and splinted it. She was busy with sutures and ants, her hands red and her face impassive. The Stonesinger had a bloodied cloth over his forehead. The Broken Witch wanted to say something to the Stonesinger's wife about head injuries but fell asleep instead.

The sleep was uneasy, filled with peculiar tensions and images from different parts of her life, jostling for attention. When she awoke hours later, everyone except Togo had gone. The Broken Witch looked around.

The cattle man knelt by his dead cow, weeping silently, his great shoulders shaking and his dark face shiny with tears. The Broken Witch found a jug beside her containing the lemon water and drank some more. She gestured to Togo to help her up and the boy did so. She leaned on Togo and gestured to the jug, which Togo managed to pick up.

They tottered towards the cow until the Broken Witch stood by the kneeling cattle man. For a while, they watched him and then the Broken Witch took the jug of lemon water from Togo and indicated he should go, giving his hand a grateful squeeze.

Eventually, the cattle man looked up. His people were not great talkers; their communication was chiefly by expression. This man's was a mixture of grief, betrayal, rage and shame. For a while, the Broken Witch stood there and then she offered the jug to the cattle man. He took the jug and drank from it. When he had had his fill, he put the jug down and looked at the cow again.

"Forgive me," the Broken Witch said.

The cattle man said nothing. His breath was ragged, and his shoulders quickly rose and fell.

"Please," the Broken Witch said. "Please."

She held out her hands but instead of taking them the man put his hands on the cow, touching her as he had when she was alive as if unable to believe she was gone. He picked up one of her broken horns and stared at it, then put it next to the jug. For a while they stayed like that.

The Broken Witch was conscious of how damaged she was, more now than before. She knew that when she ventured into the dread again it would be even harder, as if some protective layer had been stripped, like enamel from a tooth.

The cattle man looked up at her. The Broken Witch held out her hands again and the cattle man took them.

"I am sorry," the Broken Witch said.

The cattle man nodded. He touched his heart and then he touched the cow between the eyes, which he had closed. He went to say something but couldn't.

The Broken Witch took the stonesung knife from her wrap, looked at it for a moment and then held it out to the cattle man.

"For you," the Broken Witch said.

The cattle man looked astonished.

"Your father's," he said.

"Yours, now," the Broken Witch said.

The cattle man reached slowly for the stonesung knife. He

did not take it, instead running his fingertips along the smooth stone. The cattle people did not use many implements, but this one would be welcome as an heirloom and a sign of status that would enable the cattle man to regain his position. He frowned and looked up at her.

"I must go tomorrow," the Broken Witch said.

She pointed at the dread half of the village.

"Through there."

The cattle man shuddered. The Broken Witch wondered if he had stumbled into the dread as he came to find his cow. He pushed the knife back to the Broken Witch, who smiled.

"It will not help me in the dread," she said. "Indeed, I may end up using it on myself. It is better this way. Please, take it."

The cattle man took the knife and placed it next to the jug and the broken horn.

"If you would like," the Broken Witch said, "and if I return tomorrow, I will come with you to your tribe for a time and be yours and yours alone. I will heal your tribe as I do my village and you may make love with me whenever and however you wish, even in front of the others so they know how powerful you are. With me and the knife you will soon earn another cow. When you have done that I will return here to my people and every time you come past you will know where I am."

"If you come back," the cattle man said.

"Yes. It is very hard… in there. But the little girl is lost on the other side and she is my… She is Precious Child."

"Hm," the cattle man said.

He took the Broken Witch's hands in his and kissed them, one after the other. She knelt beside him and they looked at the cow with great respect. The village darkened; cooking smells began to permeate the air and the safe half of the village slowly emptied as everyone retired for dinner.

The Broken Witch was not hungry and sensed the cattle man was not either, so they stayed where they were. Eventually, the cattle man put his arm around the Broken Witch's shoulders and held them tightly. He leaned down and kissed the top of her head, where her black hair parted. He smelled her hair and kissed it and she rested her head on his shoulder, feeling his strength, letting it help her as she knew he wanted.

Presently, he moved her so that she knelt in front of him with her back to him. He eased her forward so that she rested across the cow's neck in the honoured position. Then the cattle man lifted the Broken Witch's wrap and did with her what he had wanted to do earlier.

When the Broken Witch could see again, she was naked and lying against the cattle man's chest as he rested against the curved wall of the village. Unable to speak or even think clearly, she drifted happily until the cattle man held the lemon water jug to her lips. The Broken Witch drank and would have finished it, but the cattle man laughed and pulled the jug away, swallowing the rest of lemon water himself. He put the jug down. The Broken Witch found her voice, although it was soft as old leather.

"What will you do with her?"

The cattle man looked at his cow.

"The cows give us all," he said. "Sometimes food. Her life will become mine, and yours and the village's. Other parts of her," he pointed at the broken horn, "I shall keep with me always."

The Broken Witch nodded against the cattle man's muscular chest. They lay there for a while, until the cold of the desert night began to make its way into their bodies. The Broken Witch shivered.

"I must sleep," she said. "But… Would you stay with me tonight?"

"Yes."

"The huts we use to house the tribes are empty. There is one over there we can stay in."

"Good."

"I…"

"Yes?"

"Nothing," the Broken Witch said, because she was unsure how to say what she wanted to say.

"Tribe has three watches at night," the cattle man said. "I always wake then. I have you when I wake?"

"Yes, you can have me."

"Hm."

"It is just…" She looked up at him, her lovely eyes shining in the moonlight. "I am scared."

"I will hold you. Soothe you if you dream."

The Broken Witch smiled, relieved. The cattle man eased out from behind the Broken Witch, picked up her wrap and his and slung them over his shoulders. He folded the stonesung knife and the horn into the folds of his wrap, then bent down, picked up the Broken Witch and carried her into the hut.

Steam and Power

To her surprise the Broken Witch slept through the night and woke early. She had a vague recollection of dream fragments, each the equivalent of a full screaming nightmare. Somehow, she had negotiated the ocean of sleep without fully engaging these splinters and now she was awake they receded into a distant unease.

She went to turn over and found she could not move.

The Broken Witch lay there for a while, not yet concerned. It was a long time since she had slept this deeply; perhaps her body was simply making the most of it.

The Stonesinger's wife came into the hut with a tray of food and two large stone cups with condensation glittering on their sides. They rattled against the tray because the Stonesinger's wife was shaking with fear and exhaustion, her dark skin underscored with grey and her pretty mouth trembling. She put the tray down beside the bed and sat next to it. The Broken Witch watched her, wondering if she should risk trying to speak.

"Your husband?" she managed, relieved her voice was working at least.

"He is awake and as well as can be expected. The Widow Ndugu is more concerned with the blow to the head than anything else, but my husband says it is not too bad. We feel he will recover."

The Broken Witch went to sigh with relief, but it came out as a grunt. The Stonesinger's wife gestured to the tray.

"There are two cups of very cold water that will warm up soon if you don't have them."

"Will you help me?" the Broken Witch said. "I cannot move."

The Stonesinger's wife put her face in her hands and wept.

"Arjana," the Broken Witch said. "Arjana!"

The Stonesinger's wife wiped furiously at her eyes and tried to pretend she was not crying.

"Why do you hide your tears?" the Broken Witch said. "I have known the depths of you. Stop now and look at me."

"Precious Child," the Stonesinger's wife said.

"Do you truly believe she does not mean as much to me as she does to you?" the Broken Witch said.

The Stonesinger's wife snuffled for a while, then shook her head.

The cattle man woke up. He looked around, saw the morning sunlight, the Stonesinger's wife and the breakfast. The cattle man's dazed expression drooped into disappointment at not having woken and enjoyed the Broken Witch through the night. He put his hand on her head and stroked her hair.

"Good morning," the Broken Witch said. "Help me up, will you? I cannot move."

The cattle man did so, sitting with his back to the wall of the hut with his legs spread and the Broken Witch propped between them, the back of her head resting against the big man's chest. She could hear his heart, low and strong. He made much fuss about arranging her, his hands brushing her breasts and his legs tight around her hips. She was not aware that her hair was in her eyes, but he spent some time smoothing it aside anyway. His heartbeat sped up.

The Stonesinger's wife leaned forward with one of the large cups and the Broken Witch drank from it. The icy water was delicious, and the Broken Witch finished it without spilling a drop. The Stonesinger's wife handed the other cup to the cattle man, who drank too. The Broken Witch studied the Stonesinger's wife as she leaned over.

"You tried to cross the dread in the night," the Broken Witch said.

The Stonesinger's wife busied herself with the tray of food: grain soaked in warm milk, hard-boiled eggs, crisp, bitter desert apples and some of the little figs that grew around the oasis. She pinched mixtures of food together in her strong, short fingers and held them to the lips of the Broken Witch. The Broken Witch opened her mouth and the Stonesinger's wife pushed the food in. The Broken Witch closed her lips around the fingers of the Stonesinger's wife and sucked them clean. When the Stonesinger's wife tried to ease her fingers out she found the Broken Witch had fixed her teeth on them. The Broken Witch gazed into the eyes of the Stonesinger's wife, who looked at the floor and then nodded.

"Myself and one other," the Stonesinger's wife said. "I did not get far."

The Broken Witch opened her mouth, releasing the Stonesinger's wife.

"Any dark effects?" the Broken Witch said as the Stonesinger's wife continued to feed her.

"No."

"And the other?"

"I am not sure. He kneels outside this hut, face to the ground."

"Who is it?" the Broken Witch asked, chewing.

"Adebinte. He kneels in shame and penitence. He saw you save my husband you see."

"Tell him to get up at once. If he is still grovelling when I get out there, I will kick him over the wall."

"But you cannot move, Bambomiyi."

"He does not know that. Tell him now."

The Stonesinger's wife got up and went out. The cattle man helped himself to food, devouring half the remainder before the Stonesinger's wife returned to the hut.

"Adebinte has agreed to go," she said.

"It is likely that he helped," the Broken Witch said. "Had he not stunned me with that club I would have been sensible to the dread for a lot longer."

"You were only in it for moments, Bambomiyi."

"I know."

"Can you move now?"

"No."

"Will you have more food?"

"No, thank you."

The food had seemed strange to the Broken Witch. How absurd to put these random objects through a hole in her face to mush them into a paste that was then squeezed through an array of tubes into a bag of acid. She looked down the length of her beloved body and barely recognised it.

"Perhaps the steams will revive you," the Stonesinger's wife said.

"Yes," the Broken Witch said. "And Arjana, do not let anyone else go into the dread. Only I can do it."

The Stonesinger's wife looked down the paralysed length of the Broken Witch.

"But —"

"Arjana, I am beginning to understand how this might work. There is, in me, some… thing, perhaps an aspect of my brokenness, that equips me better than anyone to undertake this journey.

"You are frustrated that a night has passed, and Precious Child is still missing, but please understand that it was important we have this time, for reasons I cannot yet explain. You have trusted me before. Trust me now."

"I trust you, Bambomiyi," the Stonesinger's wife said.

"I do, also," the cattle man said.

The cattle man slipped his arms around the Broken Witch and stood, holding her close as her legs dangled over his arms and her head rested on his shoulder. The Stonesinger's wife picked up their wraps and followed them out of the hut.

It was only the sixth hour of day and there were not many people about, so the village did not seem different. The light was rich with promise, edging the top of the wall with gold, and making the hand-sized leaves of the baduba tree glow like green flames. The cow had been covered with a sand-coloured rug.

The Stonesinger's wife followed the cattle man as he carried the Broken Witch through an opening in the wall and down, along a white tunnel and down again until they reached a series of hemispherical chambers whose walls were streaked with minerals. It was warmer in here and the air was damp. As they proceeded through the chambers, it got damper still until they reached the last, from which fragrant steam billowed like the breath of the world.

The Stonesinger's wife hung the two wraps she was carrying outside the steam chamber, then removed her own wrap and followed the cattle man in. The last chamber was darker; its curved surface patterned with complex deposits. The space was large and high, obscured from time to time by steam that sighed in through multiple vents. As it condensed across the ceiling, it accrued minerals that fell on the three people like hot, sweet rain. There were benches of different heights, pools of bubbling water at various temperatures and shelves holding cleaning devices kept sterile by the heat.

The cattle man lay the Broken Witch on her back on a high stone bench in the centre of the room and straightened her limbs. The Stonesinger's wife sat nearby with her legs curled beside her and her great ball of hair slowly drooping into hot strands around her face.

The cattle man pulled the Broken Witch's long, black hair into a rope that he lay between her spread breasts and then he crossed to the wall. Gathering a sufficient quantity of minerals in suspension, he rubbed them into the teeth and gums of the Broken Witch, holding her head still as he did so. When he had finished, he scooped cold water from a bubbling basin and poured this into the Broken Witch's mouth. She swallowed.

By now she was wet with steam, her pores open and the

previous day's dirt working its way out. The Stonesinger's wife passed a stone cleaning blade to the cattle man and the cattle man used the fine edge to wipe beads of dirt and sweat from the Broken Witch. The cattle man's face was calm but intense and the Broken Witch knew that the man had looked after his cow with the same degree of attention. The blade went across the Broken Witch's shoulders, under her arms, across her breasts and stomach, into her groin and down her thighs. The cattle man turned the Broken Witch over and worked around her neck and down her back, taking care of the Glory. He cleaned her hands, then her ankles and finally her feet.

When he was finished, he washed the blade and then used it on himself, while the Stonesinger's wife used a comb from a different shelf on the Broken Witch's hair, combing and combing until it was a shining black streak. She then rubbed minerals into it and finally sap from a covered pot. The cattle man passed the Stonesinger's wife the blade; she in turn cleaned it and then ran its edge across her own body.

The Broken Witch lay and watched the two beauties attend to their morning ritual. The sight was delightful in its innocence but had no physical effect on the Broken Witch. She could feel her clean skin tingle, her hair like a conscious thing as it drank the minerals and the sap.

She tried not to worry that her limbs were still inert.

The cattle man and the Stonesinger's wife finished cleaning and poured water over each other. Surely, *that* sight would have the Black Lion up and roaring, but no. The Broken Witch began to appreciate the cattle man's frustration at opportunities missed from sleeping through the night.

The Stonesinger's wife poured water over the Broken

Witch, first her head and then her body. The water was hot at first, then the Stonesinger's wife used cold water. The chilly shock awoke something in the Broken Witch, and she tried to cry out, but the water was everywhere, and she could not breathe —

The Realm of Knowing

The Broken Witch found herself in a curious fugue-like state. She knew she was still in the steam room with the cattle man and the Stonesinger's wife, but also existed in another place, one informed by memory as much as sensation. In the steam room her body was limp and wet, but in this other place it was dry, and she could move, alert and strong.

The tension between these two conditions was a powerful but uneasy dynamic. It allowed the Broken Witch to unconsciously assemble a whole new landscape, which she could then explore. She wondered how she was doing this; it was not something she had previously managed, or even thought possible. The dreamscape was vividly detailed, as if made up of exact memories that fitted together despite their incongruity to form a new kind of truth.

Here, for example, was the Great Hall in the Southern Realm of Knowing. The Broken Witch had been twice, once on her journey to match her outer gender with her inner, and a second, much longer stay during her training.

To the dialectic between the steam room reality and the dreamscape, was added the difference in age between her first visit and her second. The first had been at sixteen, and she was full of joyous, ruthless desperation; the second was two years later, and the Broken Witch was as calm and reasonable as she was ever going to be, in the full flowering of her youth and talent.

The Great Hall in the Realm of Knowing was a huge, spherical space at the heart of a mountain. Access was impossible for anyone not of the Way, and incredibly difficult for those who were. The Daxu had smoothed the mountain's lower flanks into a cylinder so smooth no purchase was possible, and so shiny it blinded anyone approaching with reflected sunlight. The single curved side descended into a wide chasm like a waterless moat whose floor could not be seen and from which no one had returned. The upper sections of the mountain retained some of their craggy nature, but this too had been enhanced until it resembled the barbed tip of a gigantic spear. This aspect was equally impassable; the ridges were like blades, and they were angled so the passes channelled high winds into forces of such strength nobody could hold on.

Access was via a Kani Path, and only a strong vehicle could make the journey. On her first visit, the Broken Witch had been taken by another woman like herself, on a stonesung raft with a rim the height of her forearm. The second time she had flown on her woodwing, only recently gathered from a rainforest in the centre of Zabardu. Now, as she lay motionless on the slab in the steam room, she felt again the thrill of those two journeys, and the terror.

The sense of moving, while not moving, was like what she had known in the dread. There was that same feeling of travelling fast, at great height, buffeted by invisible forces that should not exist, yet did. There was a similar feeling of being in another's hands, and at the same time flying under her own power and volition.

More potent than the dizzying perspectives of the great continent as it rushed beneath her in a tawny blur that steadied either side into broad reaches of deepest blue, more fearsome than the enlarging mountain with its daunting grey-white peaks and dazzling mirrored base, was the sense that she had already arrived, and was watching herself approach, even from within the pale rock vault of the Realm of Knowing.

The Stonesinger's wife and the cattle man seemed to be part of the landscape, as if lending their energies to its existence. The Broken Witch experienced this confusing state as an unfolding of time and space, as if to present every aspect of these two memories and her current condition in a single moment.

The Kani Path extended down into the Realm of Knowing, and access was through a series of mazes, none of which were large enough for either the raft or the woodwing. The spherical space of Realm itself was several times the width of the village in diameter. It appeared to be empty. The only things there were odd metallic protrusions – as though a gleaming steel object had exploded in the centre, and thousands of shrapnel pieces had embedded themselves in the curved wall – and, hanging unsupported in the air, ten smooth, perfectly circular stonesung discs, none thicker than the Broken Witch's finger, and each the size of the floor in the Widow Ndugu's hut. The Realm of Knowing was bright yet had no obvious source of illumination. The stonesung discs did not cast shadows, suggesting that light came from all around.

When the Broken Witch had descended into the Realm of Knowing, she had been alone each time. Now, though, she was aware of a whispering presence, and a shadow she could feel rather than see, because it was just out of sight. Had it been there then, and she did not notice it despite the clear visibility? Or was some other entity insinuating itself into this weird immersive?

The first time the Broken Witch had entered the Realm of Knowing, she had fallen sprawling onto a stone pad near the top of the great spherical chamber. Expecting the pad to bob in the air, the Broken Witch had been dismayed when the thing had not moved at all, as if it was fixed to a wall. Winded, the sixteen-year-old Broken Witch lay there and wondered what to do next.

Her second visit had lasted months, and she knew how to operate the pads because by then she had her own woodwing, formed from the seed of a huge tree and then tamed. A similar engagement to the one that flew the woodwing operated the stone pad in the Realm of Knowing, and the Broken Witch had cruised over to a metallic protrusion in the pale curved wall and touched it –

Lying in the steam room, she wondered what she had done that first time, and how she had known to do it. The two memories, and the perspectives through which she was now reliving them, had at first seemed like an unfolding. Now she noticed a stitched-together quality, as if she was suturing her damaged mind.

Through it all that strange presence whispered. Was it the dread, speaking to her? The Broken Witch thought not.

The dread was an absence, an inversion of being that did not want to destroy life, because such ambition would have required conscious will. Rather, if the dread had incorporated recognisable intelligence, then that intelligence would not have perceived life at all. This unthinking, careless and yet supremely focussed existence was, the Broken Witch realised, the most frightening aspect of the dread.

The whispering presence was not made up of the Stonesinger's wife, or the cattle man. Lying in the steam room, the Broken Witch could still sense them nearby, but they stood unmoving, mid-gesture.

The Broken Witch was aware of a silence in the steam room where none had been before. The shuffling patter of the other two people, the reassuring drip of water from the domed roof, the sigh of steam as it gusted in – all were gone. Time had either slowed or stopped completely, and the Broken Witch was experiencing her journeys on the timescale of a single thought.

The whispering voice became clearer, but the Broken Witch was still unable to make out the words. Instead, she realised it did not matter that she could not recall how she had first operated the stone pad. Perhaps the woman who took her there had explained, or perhaps the Broken Witch had learned from another Realm of Knowing. The key lay not in the instruction but the blend of selves: at sixteen, eighteen, and thirty-nine. That was the reality she had to grasp, and as she did so she understood what was happening to her.

The Daxu Touch

When the eighteen-year-old Broken Witch touched the gleaming protrusion in the Realm of Knowing, she tumbled into a silvery vortex.

Information flowed around and through her; some she understood and some she did not. How, for example, was she still alive? She had been in the Realm of Knowing for six weeks, had not eaten or drunk anything, and yet felt no diminution of strength or metabolism. Could her engagements with the Realm be sustaining her, perhaps by transmitting the required energies for life directly into her body? The Broken Witch did not know. She simply understood that in six weeks she had absorbed an incredible amount of knowledge.

Twenty-one years later, lying on the slab in the village steam room and trying not to think about Precious Child lost in the dread, the Broken Witch wondered why these details were coming back to her now. Why was she recalling this engagement with the Realm of Knowing, out of the many she had undertaken there?

The shadow beside her deepened, and the whispering grew louder…

In the Realm of Knowing, the Broken Witch's mind

plunged on through the vortex while her body remained back in the spherical chamber, lying on a smooth stone disc in the same way as her older body lay in the steam room. She was thus removed from herself two, even three times and in that separation a new calm blossomed, easing the devastating effects of the dread.

The first time the Broken Witch had engaged with the Realm of Knowing in this manner it terrified her. Most overwhelming was seeing and moving in all directions, as if her mind was enlarging to the size of a world. Then there was the sense of being *added to*, as though tiny silver grains of information were being seeded through her, linking and then growing into a web that pulsed with glittering power.

In her spaced-out condition, the Broken Witch realised that the dread did the opposite. Those grains of silver magic were long gone, but the process of stripping her back, as though with an acid mist, was horribly similar to what happened in the war, when –

She almost had it then, and if she had been able to move would have hissed with frustration.

Instead, the whispering grew louder, and the shadow became a shape, a figure she recognised: a slim, improbably busty dark-skinned woman with long shiny black hair that looked wrong but still suited her, in a multicoloured wrap. The Broken Witch knew then that the dread did not change time; it changed her perception of it. That was what these memories were for, to create an overlapping self to fill in the blanks, to… to *heal*.

This odd fugue, with its timeless vistas and vivid, blended recollections was like a bruise in the mind from the dread's onslaught – a rush of ideas and memories to counter that lethal touch of the void. The Broken Witch realised that she would be able to undertake the journey across the village; that in some respects it had already begun. It would, she understood, be even harder than she had imagined, not least because of what she must face within herself.

Her shadow aspect smiled, leaned forward, and whispered a name.

A Gathering Plan

In the village steam room, the Broken Witch gasped and sat up. The Stonesinger's wife stroked the Broken Witch's wet hair and touched her face.

"Bambomiyi?" she said.

The cattle man knelt and put an arm around the Broken Witch's shoulders.

"Pretty witch?" the cattle man said.

"Basu," the Broken Witch said.

She looked up at the cattle man, then with effort turned her head to look at the Stonesinger's wife.

"My name," the Broken Witch said, "is Basu, after my father, who ever after was known as Large Basu."

"Yes," the Stonesinger's wife said.

"Yes," the cattle man said.

The Broken Witch breathed deeply. A smile spread across her face. Her large hands with their elegant fingers flexed, then flexed again.

"You can both let go now," the Broken Witch said.

The Stonesinger's wife and the cattle man did so and stepped away. The Broken Witch rolled onto her side and slid her legs to the floor. For a while she stayed like that, her breathing deep, then eased herself upright.

"Basu," she said. "Yes."

The other two got to their feet.

"More cold water," the Broken Witch said.

They poured it over her and kept pouring; some she drank, and the rest splashed down her, snapping shut her pores and rushing down her hair. Within the torrent, she growled.

Finally, she walked out of the water as the cattle man was pouring it and strode into the adjoining chamber. The cattle man put down the bucket and followed with the Stonesinger's wife.

The Broken Witch took down her wrap and carried it through the chambers, whose atmospheres dried her. As she reached the last, she put on her wrap and the cattle man and the Stonesinger's wife did the same. The Broken Witch turned to them.

"We must go up onto the wall and survey the village, so I can examine the route," she said.

"The quickest way onto the wall is through here," the Stonesinger's wife said.

She went up several flights of steps and out onto the curved top of the village wall. The Broken Witch followed her, and the cattle man came last. They stood in the sun, which drew the last of the steam room's moisture from them.

The rocky desert lumbered west in glorious silence past the high green spread of the oasis to a range of mountains purpled by great hot distance. In the other direction, the sandy desert moved its great mass about with infinitesimal care. The dunes marched steadily at geological speed, their pace no less impressive in its way than that of the small, spotted lions whose chasing velocity rendered them hard to see.

Between the two worlds was the village, set back from the crossroads of the two Kani Paths.

The Broken Witch, the Stonesinger's wife and the cattle man gazed down at the large circular space, dotted with huts and held by the white arms of the wall. The line through the centre was scuffed even more, thanks to the Broken Witch and the cow.

There was another, much more troubling detail.

"What is that?" the Broken Witch asked.

"Another line," the Stonesinger's wife said.

"The dread grows?" the cattle man said.

The Stonesinger's wife nodded.

"About a foot last night," she said. "We found out when Adebinte tried to cross and went mad before he reached the line."

"One thing at a time," the Broken Witch said. "Where was Precious Child when you saw her last?"

The Stonesinger's wife pointed to the far side of the village.

"What was she doing?" the Broken Witch said.

"Playing. She decided she was going to put on that lion costume you got her last year. I said no. It was too hot and anyway the costume is tatty because she always wears it. We had a few cross words. She said she was going to get the costume but not put it on and I said that was all right; anything to avoid one of those tempers she has never quite grown out of…"

The Stonesinger's wife stopped talking and her chest heaved for a while. The Broken Witch and the cattle man watched, calm and patient. The Stonesinger's wife waved a hand although the gesture's significance was not clear.

"Did she get the costume?" the Broken Witch asked.

"She went to get it," the Stonesinger's wife said.

"From where? Your home?"

"No. Her friend, Bipe's. Precious Child had lent it to her because Bipe's mother has gone with the woodsinger tribe to trade in the south west and Bipe misses her."

"Where does Bipe live?"

The Stonesinger's wife pointed.

"In that hut?" the Broken Witch said.

"No, the cave beyond."

"Where is Bipe now?"

"She and her father are with us here. Precious Child was not with them and they had not seen her when they came."

"Did they have the lion costume?"

"No."

"Precious Child may have it. She could have got it from Bipe and put it on away from you so you would not see."

"You think so?"

"It is what I would have done," the Broken Witch said.

Tears ran down the face of the Stonesinger's wife, but her voice was steady.

"I think you are right," she said.

"How did the dread arrive?" the Broken Witch said.

"It began as a feeling of unease," the Stonesinger's wife said. "A worry we could not place. We thought there was bad weather coming, but none of the signs were there. We thought there might be a sickness, but there were no signs of that either and you would have known before anyone."

"Yes," the Broken Witch said. "I sensed nothing."

"We thought perhaps there were bad people about, like those raiders who came last year." She frowned. "What became of them?"

"Better you do not know," the Broken Witch said.

"Hm," the Stonesinger's wife said. "Anyway, it was none of those things but felt like a mix of all, at the same time. We came out into the village circle, and everyone was talking at once. There were arguments that would have got violent but did not because anger became a kind of tiredness that was somehow still enervating. We noticed the other side of the village seemed normal; no one there was arguing, or out in the circle."

The Stonesinger's wife shuddered.

"We suddenly had to get over to the safe side of the village. There was not even any discussion. Everyone was in our half of the circle and then, like a rush, we all ran to the other side. There was no thought, only movement. Such was the imperative that we did not even think Precious Child was not with us. Why would she have stayed there, in that?"

The Broken Witch tried to keep the bleakness off her face.

"You say that you came out into the circle of the village," the Broken Witch said. "Where did you come from?"

"My husband was in his workshop. I was about to have my hair done, then get fruit for dinner... Oh."

The cattle man swallowed.

"It is beyond the circle of the village," he said. "In the caves and tunnels."

"That is where Precious Child is," the Stonesinger's wife whispered.

"It might already have engulfed her," the Broken Witch said.

The Stonesinger's wife convulsed and would have leaped off the top of the wall like her husband if the Broken Witch had not seized her and swung her away. The Stonesinger's wife became hysterical and the Broken Witch held her at arm's length for a time.

"Arjana," she said.

The Stonesinger's wife ran out of energy and slumped. The Broken Witch held her up and then shook her, hard.

"You think I have time to rescue you as well?" the Broken Witch shouted. "How are you helping Precious Child by killing yourself? We must use our minds!"

The Stonesinger's wife appeared senseless.

"Arjana please, I need your help," the Broken Witch said. "I cannot do this without you."

The Stonesinger's wife sighed, so deep and mournful it was hard to hear.

"If she is in… *that*… If she still lives… She might be mad by now."

"Yes," the Broken Witch said. "She might be."

For a while they stood and allowed the truth of it.

"But we simply do not know," the Broken Witch said. "And if she is mad, there are things that can be done. You cannot give up now."

Eventually, the Stonesinger's wife nodded. She looked up at the Broken Witch and touched her face.

"Forgive me," the Stonesinger's wife said.

"I may," the Broken Witch said. "I may not."

Despite herself, the Stonesinger's wife smiled and they

turned again to the village.

"Can I go around the top of the wall?" the Broken Witch said.

"No," the Stonesinger's wife said. "That is what my husband tried. If the dread is beneath the wall on the bad side of the village, it must be above it as well. That is why he fell."

The Broken Witch pointed to the centre of the village.

"How many paces from the new line to the far side?" the Broken Witch said.

"A hundred," the cattle man said.

"Yes," the Stonesinger's wife said.

"That is what I think, also," the Broken Witch said.

"Through the dread," the Stonesinger's wife said.

"An impossible journey," the cattle man said.

"From one side of the village to the other," the Broken Witch said, and chuckled.

The cattle man made a strange sound, as if he was sneezing. He put his hand to his eyes and the women realised the big man was crying.

"Stop that now," the Broken Witch said. "I am the one everybody should feel sorry for, not you."

"My pretty witch," the cattle man said.

He put his arms around the Broken Witch and held her. After a while, the Broken Witch spoke from within the firm, tender embrace.

"You will not let go, will you?"

The cattle man shook his head. The Broken Witch slipped free and looked up at him.

"Now," she said. "I cannot be worrying about you, any more than I can be worrying about her," she nodded towards the Stonesinger's wife. "I want you to look after your dear cow and send her on her way, which will take much work."

The cattle man sniffled.

"It will," he said.

"Arjana will help you," the Broken Witch said. "However, she is a married woman, so do not go getting any ideas."

"Hm," the cattle man said.

"When I get back with Precious Child, I will be most annoyed if that cow is still there," the Broken Witch said.

The other two nodded.

"I think that is all," the Broken Witch said.

She turned and then turned back.

"If I fall and do not get up, leave me. In fact, whatever happens, do not interfere. Should I fail, you must all leave the village. Tell the Headmun in such a way that he thinks it is his idea, then make it so and do it fast.

"We are a practical people. We will always do well."

The Broken Witch did not wait for a response. She went down the steps, through the wall and out onto the circle. Ahead, the crudely drawn line stretched from one side of her vision to the other. Beyond it, the scuffed first line was a frightening echo.

"Basu," the Broken Witch said to herself. "And Large Basu."

She crossed the space through the other villagers, who had begun to gather.

"Are you going then, Bambomiyi?"

"Yes."

"We wish you well, Bambomiyi."

"Thank you."

"Sorry for hitting you with my club, Bambomiyi."

"I will get you for that, Adebinte."

"Bambomiyi?"

The Broken Witch turned and saw the Headmun with the Widow Ndugu behind him.

"Can we help in any way?" the Headmun said.

"Yes," the Broken Witch said. "Go about your business and pay no heed to what happens in the dread."

"We will do it," the Headmun said. "Remember what I told you before."

"The love of the village is my greatest weapon," the Broken Witch said.

She looked past the Headmun at the Widow Ndugu, whose face was without expression as usual. However, she raised her hand, its back towards the Broken Witch: the threat of a blow, the kind the Broken Witch enjoyed. The Broken Witch laughed, and the Headmun and the Widow Ndugu moved off.

The village bustled around the Broken Witch as it always did. It pleased her to know that this perilous quest was merely part of an ordinary day.

The Broken Witch checked her palms and was pleased to find they were not sweating. She smoothed her wrap although it did not need it and ran her fingers through her hair, which felt smooth and warm in the morning sunlight. There was nothing more to do.

She breathed once, breathed twice, and stepped across the line.

This Dark Bargain

The dread was much worse this time. Either it was growing in power or damage had rendered the Broken Witch more vulnerable.

There was a sense of imminent disaster, already too late to avert, like knowledge of an injury or illness whose effects have yet to be felt.

It was that awful moment in which everything is thrown into the terrible perspective of its own demise.

That awful moment, stretched into an age.

The Broken Witch stood just across the border, aware she had taken but one step of a hundred and was already annihilated.

The dread made everything into itself, yet still enabled gloomy echoes of recollection, so its victims knew themselves as such but were helpless to do anything about it.

The Broken Witch went to use her strength, but it was gone. She wanted to shout, but no sound came. She tried to think of Precious Child and the Stonesinger's wife; of the cattle man and the Widow Ndugu, but they were dark smudges against a blinding light.

Basu.
Yes.
Bambomiyi.
Yes.
Broken Witch.
Oh, yes.

My broken selves.
My shattered life.

This is the way forward.
The dread cannot destroy that which is already destroyed.

Ha.

The Broken Witch took another step.

It seemed vast, this undertaking, as if the Broken Witch was as tall as the sky and every step a force that shattered continents.

That must be why she felt such vertigo, fearing impact less than the instant of falling, when something could still be done, if only, if only…

The vertigo swirled through her.

She had never felt so sick.

The Broken Witch had known illness in most of its forms. However, there had never been anything like this.

This was a city-killing plague, condensed into one body.

It was a thing that could end species.

There was no way out; certainly not into madness, because it was madness that surrounded and suffused her, quiet and lethal.

Had she not healed, though, herself and others, many times?

You broke your promise, witch, and that is why you are broken.

Whose voice was that?

She listened, but there was only silence.

What promise?

A problem to solve distracted the Broken Witch enough to take another step.

As her foot landed, she fell back in time.

*

"You know the price for desertion, Basu."

Another voice now: older, female. The threat in her flat tone was underscored with compassion, which made it even more frightening. It was a familiar voice, although one the Broken Witch believed she had forgotten, the memory blasted out of her by… by…

"My father is sick."

The Broken Witch recognised her own voice. How sure of herself she sounded!

"We are ten thousand miles from your village, Basu. The message about your father would have taken a long time to reach us here in the north. Even along the Kani Paths, it is unlikely you will get there in time."

The voice took on more texture like an echo coming closer, losing resonance. Fragments of image slowly coalesced, as if the dread was a storm blowing sand from some deeply buried structure.

She recognised the feel of something around her – not a wrap; something alive and attuned to her, its outline her own. The colour of desert sand at dusk, the chitinous garment had leathery joints for supple movement and was vulnerable only to the most powerful weapons of the Way.

It was studded with blade-like bones which it discarded like teeth: daggers and knives in pockets down the front, swords in sheathes at either hip and down her back. The ones at the Broken Witch's back were short enough to be drawn with ease but long enough for the bony handles to jut either side of her head. Throwing stars edged with venom waited in discrete pouches.

The sand-coloured garment was a setatu, named after the armoured beetle. It protected the Broken Witch in battle as she fought her way to injured warriors, whom she would pull from the carnage and carry to her woodwing.

The Broken Witch was a chiyembekazo. Often shortened to 'kazo', it was a name from the other end of Zabardu that meant 'hope'.

The woman who sat before the Broken Witch was in her fifties, her hair woven into the complex pattern denoting her senior rank. She wore grey lightstone armour, its marbled surface a striking contrast to her dark, lined skin. The armour was from the time of the Daxu and did not quite fit. The Broken Witch knew that the impenetrable lightstone shielding weighed less than the setatu, which weighed almost nothing.

The woman sat in a carved wooden chair. She had used a woodsung one before, but it had been lost when the enemy's firedancers attacked a supply convey along the great Kani

Path of the Western Coast. This chair was cruder than the old one. It spoke of disappointment, of Daxu bloodlines diluted in the frantic human tide that followed their departure.

The small tent the two women spoke in was indistinguishable from others in the camp. It was a practical measure: clever and yet somehow too accommodating, as if lacking in confidence.

There was no one else present, and the Broken Witch stood with her fists clenched at her sides.

"I must try, Thema," the Broken Witch said, her voice tight with anger.

"You are one of three remaining kazo," Thema said.

"Four."

"Lusala got an axe through her yesterday."

The Broken Witch gasped in horror. Lusala had been the best of them; the Broken Witch had thought Lusala indestructible.

"How?"

"The enemy is led by an exceptional warrior. He is of the Way, with the Daxu blood strong in him."

"Is he big, whiter even than the others, with long, black hair and a sword that shines red?"

"You have seen him, then."

"Yes," the Broken Witch said. "And he killed Lusala?"

"It is hard to say," Thema said. "We have an accord with the enemy that allows you kazo to carry out your duty and theirs to do the same. However, ours are fewer and we started with more."

"We started with twenty," the Broken Witch said, not bothering to hide the accusation.

"Hm," Thema said, feigning nonchalance. "I believe this

warrior has enabled the killing, while not actually doing it himself."

"You want me to kill him," the Broken Witch said.

"Yes."

"You think I will succeed where others have failed because I am a kazo and the enemy will not expect an attack from me."

"Yes."

"And then you will let me go to my father."

"Yes."

"Although as a kazo I am not permitted to kill like that. It is against my oath, against the source of my power, everything —"

"I know what it is against," Thema said.

The Broken Witch saw then how ruthless the other woman was. How could she be anything else? This war had been going on for a generation.

The Broken Witch thought of Large Basu. It had always been just the two of them, and the Broken Witch regarded her father as an even greater source of power than the Way. The Way was so hard to engage; its physical, intellectual and spiritual requirements were overwhelming and yet its entirety was forever out of reach. Large Basu made no such demands.

"Outside the Choice I have never killed anyone, Sika," the Broken Witch said, using the chief's formal title without quite knowing why.

"I know, Basu," Thema said.

Her voice was gentle and her eyes sad. She knew full well what she was asking.

"What will be the effect on me if I do this thing?" the Broken Witch asked.

"We do not know," Thema said. "I have enquired, and it is likely you will not be affected; that you will still be able to engage the Way to save Large Basu."

"He has the blood sickness," the Broken Witch said. "I cannot afford any diminution of my ability."

"I do not believe it will happen," Thema said. "The kazo prohibition against murder is a moral decision, not one that involves the Way."

Says one who never has and never could experience it, the Broken Witch thought.

"You must decide now," Thema said. "It is unusual that a battle lasts this long. We are due to recommence, and I fully expect the enemy to attack before the agreed time."

This eagerness in Thema was peculiar and the Broken Witch could not stop herself frowning. What was Thema not telling her?

"Basu!" Thema urged.

The Broken Witch thought of her father, lying in the domed chamber beyond his workshop, his chest rising and falling quicker than it should, his powerful frame diminished. He expected nothing; his generosity extended to warriors he had never met, whose welfare was his child's duty. The message from the village had come from the Headmun, not Large Basu.

The Broken Witch knew there was more to it. Thema's uncharacteristic anxiety enhanced a sense in the Broken Witch of her own repressed unease and the unacknowledged guilt beneath. The combination made her jumpy and over-eager for resolution.

"Has he a name, this warrior?" the Broken Witch said.

Thema formed the word in the enemy's tongue with difficulty.

"Feros."

The Broken Witch nodded.

"I will kill Feros," she said.

Belly of a Monster

The Broken Witch surged back into the present. The conversation with Thema had been recollected with such intensity that it warded off awareness of the dread. Now, though, the Broken Witch saw she had barely covered a quarter of the distance across the village.

She was curled up on her side, gritty dust from the ground in her mouth, her body assailed by weird pain that felt like nothing yet hurt more than any battle wound. The ground seemed to be trying to throw her off with the force of a quake and the silence of that falling sensation on the cusp of sleep. The bright sky felt black, yet still dazzled, the ground formed of a hundred thousand tiny barbed mountains like the one that guarded the Southern Realm of Knowing.

To the predations of the dread was added a new and thunderous sense of loss. The Broken Witch had numbed herself to the loss of her setatu, to the extent that its name was as lost to her as her own. Yet now she remembered: the setatu was female, and her name was Sila.

Sila had grown with the Broken Witch in the ancient kazo temple in the rainforest. The setatu began as a pale leather strip that wound itself about the Broken Witch's waist and stayed there, easing its spiky intelligence into her dreams and growing around her, week after week and month after month until witch and armour were almost a single being.

Without Sila, the Broken Witch suddenly felt that her skin was missing; that she lay on the harsh, gritty floor of the village with every nerve and tissue exposed and sharp stones pressing into the open wounds. The dread amplified this physical and emotional agony and the Broken Witch writhed, making it even worse.

Only a broken witch could have survived it. Already weakened, she had known madness in herself and others, understood the terrain a mind travels under such duress. She had come back from endless war and knew how to fight, and that the essence of conflict is not the rush of bravado at the outset but the long, slow, impossible slog when strength and courage are gone and only will remains: the will to victory over the enemy, but first over herself.

Her defiant scream may have emerged as a squeak, her leap into action may have been a clumsy roll onto her side, her ingenious strategy may have been the slow shuffle to her knees, and her victory the creaking leverage to a standing position, but each of these achievements in the heart of the dread was a triumph, each an inspiration to drive her on, to somehow do it all again.

She looked around, but nothing she saw made any sense. The leaves of the baduba tree were higher from the ground than the top of the cattle man's head, but the Broken Witch could see them in front of her. Yet when she waved her hand at the leaves, her fingers touched only air. The village wall should have been far away, but appeared to be to her left, and not a curve at all but a long strip, as if part of it had been chopped out and put beside her. Again, when she reached for it, she found nothing. When she looked down, she saw the sky.

The Broken Witch squeezed her eyes shut, and when she opened them, the view was even more confusing. The wreck was there, but it was smaller than her, and she could see a curious weathering on the spire, as though sparks had carved dark channels through the uncanny wood. How could she know that such marks existed? She had never climbed the wreck or seen the spire up close. The lower part looked wrong, and the Broken Witch recognized that it had become Thema's chair, and then, beyond, she saw Thema's face, the size of the village wall. Thema's eyes were huge with terror, but she was speaking calmly. The Broken Witch could not hear Thema's words but knew from the way her lips writhed and struggled that she was speaking a language neither of them knew.

The Broken Witch was sure she was stationary, but everything around her was in motion, as though she was moving at many speeds simultaneously. Fragments came at her, receded, and superimposed themselves over each other. The fragments were memories of the village throughout her life, and of different places entirely. She tried to make out a pattern in the giddying whirl of images, but there was none.

It was as if the chronological distortions in her mind had caused a delay between what she saw and how she interpreted it. The delay was not constant, so different images reached her at different times in different ways.

As well as the pummelling psychological onslaught, the

dread had begun to refract the Broken Witch's reality, and she was lost in a storm. If she got turned around, she would spend longer in it than even she could withstand. Her mind would collapse, and she would die before she could reach Precious Child.

If she could only be sure she was pointed in the right direction! Her limbs were drained of strength, but they still reluctantly obeyed her. If she could move a few steps, or even one step, perhaps the nightmare would settle, or present some perspective she could use to get a bearing.

Yet it was impossible. The zooming vistas around her multiplied and rebounded upon themselves, and the Broken Witch knew that her balance would pack up soon as her mind tried to orient her in the impossible space. Even closing her eyes did not help, because she was still trying to make sense of what she had just seen, and her crazed vision continued regardless.

She made the mistake of hesitating, and then she fell.

Hitting the ground was such agony it almost snuffed her out. One sensation that had been constant was the exposed-nerve rawness of Sila's loss, so each speck of dust turned her flesh into an abrading shroud. This harsh smothering cut at the Broken Witch with so much brute and blunted fury that the terrified animal within her found the strength to scream: a long, high note almost cathartic in its purity.

Like anyone, the Broken Witch tended to hunch up or gather herself together after injury, to protect the wounded area. Now, however, everything was back to front, so instead she stretched, feeling the wrongness of it yet powerless to do anything except reach her limbs across the cruel ground as if she was trying to wrench herself apart.

Her fingertips touched something. It was smooth, with a gradual curve that suggested a broad, squat stonesung cylinder. The Broken Witch spread her hot palm across the surface, which extended up. She waited for the sensations to become confused, but they did not. The cool finish remained pressed against her trembling hand, and she inched towards it across the lacerating ground, her teeth chattering with pain.

Soon, she was close enough to lever her upper body off the ground and lean her cheek to the wall. She spread her shaking arms across the surface, as if embracing it. Her left fingers hooked around a straight vertical edge, then something brushed against the back of her hand and moved as it swung slightly on hinges. A wooden door.

She had reached a hut, but which one was it?

The Broken Witch forced her tormented mind to calm and considered the problem. Some huts had wooden doors but not all, because wood was rare. Others had curtains, some had stonesung doors and some huts had nothing at all. The variables were still too many, however. The Broken Witch could easily end up orbiting the hut until her soul gave out.

In the centre of her brilliant mind, where the vestiges of rationality cowered, she managed a calculation unencumbered by agony and fear. Before the storm closed in, she had seen how she was a quarter of the way across the village, in a direct route from where she had started, bisecting the line that demarcated the dread. That meant the Widow Ndugu's hut was directly behind her. Only one hut was opposite that, and it had a wooden door. It was Adebinte's hut.

The Broken Witch knew which way the door faced. She

gripped the edge and pulled herself forward, her voice too ragged now to scream or even cry out. Bracing herself, she used all her Daxu strength to get upright. It still took her an age, as did the gradual inching across the doorway and around the wall, using her hands to measure the way.

She kept her eyes closed, which meant no fresh images accosted her. Slowly, the visual storm eased into a pulse of memories, insistent yet thankfully vague. The Broken Witch had known military discipline and employed it now to remember the view from Adebinte's hut to the far wall. She focussed and focussed until she could see it as if it was there before her, and then she stepped forward.

The Kani Paths of War

The battle was a living stain below her. It seethed and grew, changing shape and colour. The smells of burnt blood, metal and excrement reached her, even suspended as she was in the upper reaches of the Kani Path. She had chosen her usual height of two-hundred feet above the fighting; always a tricky decision and dependent on the nature of the battle. This one had fewer archers on both sides after yesterday's slaughter, so the risk of an arrow through the head was diminished.

Around her, the grassland plain stretched off in all directions; the flat, even ground perfect for fighting. It was early morning. The sun was bright, but a cooling wind blew from the west; it flowed around the Broken Witch's armour, moved the tight, black ball of her hair and rustled the leaves of the woodwing.

The woodwing was a complex of interwoven, gnarled wood in the shape of two slim spindles, one in front of the other. The Broken Witch was stretched across the top of these structures and fitted snugly against them. Her midsection rested on the joint between the spindles and her legs were hooked into the swelling at the rear to prevent her falling off.

Her hands were inside the front spindle gripping two woody knobs, one each side of a central trunk. Thorns behind these protrusions and under the Broken Witch's wrists sometimes grew into her flesh to replenish the blood connection, but they were quiescent now.

Leaves of every shape and colour sprouted along the rear spindle, lending the woodwing a festive look. The leaves could adapt to the physiognomy of the wounded to regrow flesh and bone and dissemble infection, while sap in the wood could be consumed to address every ailment of human and Daxu.

A sense of alarm: spears, coming at her! Four of them, hurled by warriors of the Way; only they could get a spear this high at that speed. The Broken Witch eased back in the woodwing saddle and slid the two swords from their sheaths on her back. She cut the first two spears out of the sky; they fell in pieces to the floor of the Kani Path as the Broken Witch engaged the woodwing in a process faster than thought and spun aside. The last two spears flew past her and arced to the plain below.

The Broken Witch banked left along the Kani Path, dropping in silence until she skimmed the ground just behind the senior ranks of the Zabardan army. They paid her little heed; their focus was on the fighting.

The battle had been underway for seven minutes. Thema's battle group should have been committed across a third of the north-west region, including a city and the port the enemy used as its headquarters. However, Thema had concentrated the bulk of her military strength on the current battle. The enemy was thus outnumbered but possessed uncanny weapons the Zabardan army lacked.

The worst of these were the steeds: ostensibly armoured mounts, but savage fighting creatures in themselves. The things were like giant demon horses crossed with a hybrid of human and wolf. Red-eyed, fanged and with retractable five-inch claws, their shaggy coats deflected all but the strongest sword thrust and yet failed to overheat the monster beneath. Steeds ran so fast it was hard to see them and the only advantage for the Zabardans was that when the steeds were running they weren't fighting. Able to rear up on their hind legs with the same balance as a human, steeds used their great height and formidable claws to stab and slash. They were creatures of the Way, but not very clever; they were instead engaged in the same fashion that the Broken Witch engaged her woodwing. Fortunately, there were not many steeds; the Broken Witch had counted thirty of them, which was twelve less than yesterday.

The worst of the steeds was ridden by Feros, who had not yet appeared on the field.

Thema's strategy was to push the enemy south and then force them west onto the crossroads of another two Kani Paths, using a reserve force hidden behind baffles on the eastern plain. This crossroads was about half a mile from the one now engaged by the Broken Witch and would be known to the enemy. Weapons of the Way were at their most potent along the Kani Paths; the invaders would become desperate and unpredictable if they intuited Thema's plan.

The Broken Witch could do little about any of it, except strike the moment she saw Feros. Where was he?

The Broken Witch rose above the battle again. No further attack on her materialised; whoever had thrown those spears was now either dead or otherwise occupied. It was just as well, because now the Broken Witch had to make the Choice.

She must descend into the fighting and determine who could be saved and who could not, who could be attended to on the battlefield and who must be carried to the healing camp half a mile down the Kani Path. She must then enable that decision because there was no longer anyone else. The other kazo was running the healing camp after its original chief died from exhaustion; the third was in reserve.

However, it was not workload that made the Choice insufferable, it was that the Broken Witch must choose who to save from those she had marched with, got drunk with, made love to, fallen out with, made up with and healed of the myriad idiotic injuries suffered by any army at any time.

It never got easier. It was not possible for it to get worse.

She saw where the fighting was at its most intense, calculated the distance, noted the weapons in play and the likeliest resulting injuries, pulled appropriate leaves and sap from the woodwing and wove them into the setatu.

She engaged the Way.

The woodwing shot up and then dropped, reaching maximum velocity above the heads of the Zabardan senior ranks. The Broken Witch kicked her booted feet loose and catapulted off the woodwing, right on the edge of the Kani Path.

The Broken Witch went headfirst, feet tight together and arms at her sides. She flew over her seniors and the mounted reserves, over the remains of the archers and the first of the fighting. She flew over a steed that pawed at her, its claws just missing her belly. She flew over the dead and dying on the bloodied grass; over the terror-frozen and traumatised; over screaming and silence and the shit-stink of terror, right into the worst of it.

The Broken Witch curled into a ball and bounced off the flank of a steed. The beast was hard but pliable, like a reptile but hot, so hot. Its horrible face turned to her, fangs dripping red.

The Broken Witch had both side swords out, feet apart and ready. The double-edged blades were two feet long, their points and edges so sharp they were almost insubstantial. The Broken Witch engaged the Way again; the blades hummed along the rough handles and glowed bright in the morning sun.

The steed went for her with both sets of front claws; the Broken Witch parried one and sheared four claws right off. The steed snarled, a low sound with a dark beauty of its own. The Broken Witch felt the snarl resonate within her, rippling the calm she relied on to stay alive. The steed nearly took her face off and the Broken Witch ducked, conscious she had lost some essential rhythm in the encounter.

The steed bunched its damaged claw into a fist and slammed it into the Broken Witch's side. The setatu absorbed some of the impact and the Broken Witch leapt sideways away from the blow to lessen it. Her ribs didn't shatter, but she was still in agony as she slammed face down into steaming entrails.

The steed leaped, its back claws aiming for the Broken Witch's head. Spitting slimy guts that tasted of snot and metal, she rolled aside and as the steed landed the Broken Witch sliced off one of its back legs. The thing screeched and as it leaned back on its remaining limbs the Broken Witch rammed both swords into the belly. Hissing blood spray told the Broken Witch she'd got the heart; she pulled out the swords, danced back and decapitated the steed before it collapsed on her.

The armoured rider cried out and clutched his head as the link with his mount was broken. The rider spoke in the strange, high piping language of the invaders and the Broken Witch could hear the words broken by sobs as the beast slumped to the ground. The rider did not even care that the Broken Witch stood before him, bloodied swords still in her hands. It was an easy matter for her to re-engage one of her blades and touch the rider's neck with the point, rendering him unconscious. She turned from the fallen steed and its rider, crouching low and holding her blades parallel with the ground.

Around her was the familiar, oddly muted noise of battle: the thud of footfall and hoof beat; the clash and crack of weaponry. Grunting, sobbing, panting; the sound of people at the heart of something, where it is never wholly clear what is going on.

Fortunately, the enemy was unmistakable. Their shape was like the Zabardans although slenderer, as if attenuated by the chill of their far northern realm. They were horribly, unnaturally *white*, their eyes creepy shades of blue and green. No human should look like that, especially in the bright morning sun that slowly reddened exposed northern flesh. Their hair was weird as well. Some of the northern Zabardans had straight hair, but it was always black; never brown, red, or *yellow*! Ugh. Monsters, then, whatever strange beauty could be parsed from their unwholesome appearance.

They were here for the weeping steel, which came only

from Zabardu and for which the Zabardans had no use; indeed, were happy to give away in return for stonework or designs for those odd machines the northerners brought. But the northerners were greedy; they wanted more and more, rucking up the precious landscape in their frantic, desperate search. Hence this unending, stupid war.

"Basu."

The male voice was familiar, but the Broken Witch couldn't place it or tell the direction from whence it came. She stayed crouched as a riderless horse thundered past.

Four feet away, two women attacked a man: the women's dark brown skin almost black against their opponent's. He was deft, with a single blade of some glimmering metal that felled one of the women before the other leaped over the sword and drove a stone knife into the man's head. He fell without a cry.

The Broken Witch crept over to over the fallen woman, whose companion had disappeared. The woman was still alive; her eyelids flickered as she clutched her stomach. The Broken Witch sheathed one sword and kept the other loose as she pried the woman's hands away. The woman whimpered.

The wound was terrible; the sword had gone straight through, severing the woman's spine and rupturing her lower organs, their contents now spreading and becoming toxic. There was nothing the Broken Witch could do, except assist with parting.

Pulling a throwing star from its pouch, the Broken Witch touched the point to the woman's neck. The woman gasped, her pain becoming pleasure and then deep sleep. The Broken Witch held the warrior as she passed, then laid her down.

"Basu!"

Where was that voice coming from?

Something hit the Broken Witch in the back, and she sprawled over the dead woman. Rolling over, she saw that a giant, looming figure of indeterminate gender had tried to run her through with a spear, only to be frustrated by the setatu. The Broken Witch pulled a dagger from the armour on her chest and hurled it into her attacker's neck. The attacker went down, the dagger still embedded. It would come out eventually and leave no mark, assuming the giant warrior was not trampled in the meantime.

"Basu…"

The Broken Witch dodged a blow from some ghastly metal ball studded with spikes that would have cleanly removed her head. The invaders were full of sadistic invention; it would be exciting were the Broken Witch not so sick of it. Perhaps killing Feros would end the conflict; one great evil preventing a multitude of lesser ones.

The Broken Witch cut through the chain attached to the ball, then kicked the attacker in the chest. He flew back, hit a Zabardan horse galloping in the other direction and bounced at the Broken Witch again, who knocked him out with a punch to the chin.

The Broken Witch moved on, finding her rhythm now as she danced through the battle.

She dispensed a dozen reviving jabs for shock, hysteria or madness and used thirty woodwing leaves on lacerations of varying severity. She amputated a total of eighteen arms, cauterised the stumps and used a serum to send the dazed warriors sprinting to the healing camp through the battle so fast no one could touch them. She amputated three legs;

one warrior died, and the others had to be hauled off to the healing field on the woodwing. The Broken Witch gave another merciful release, then another. She fixed spilled guts, pushed them back in and sealed them inside. Six gutted warriors were flown to the healing camp but eight could not be moved. She had to leave them unconscious, hoping they would be mistaken for the dead.

There was still no sign of Feros.

A hand grasped the Broken Witch's leg and she looked down.

"Makena!" she said.

The man smiled up, teeth red with his blood.

"Was it you calling?" the Broken Witch said.

"Yes," Makena said. "Seeing you kept me alive."

"No, keeping pressure on that wound like I told you after last time kept you alive."

The Broken Witch ducked as an arrow flew over her head and embedded itself in the chest of a man with hair the colour of sunset. He looked at the Broken Witch and tried to speak; instead, his eyes rolled back as he sat cross-legged and stayed there.

"You have saved many today, Basu," Makena said.

"I have lost count. Quiet, now."

Makena was cut through between the chest and left shoulder. The invader responsible lay face down nearby, helmed head at a strange angle. The wound in Makena's front bubbled bloodily; a lung had been punctured. There was more: Makena was limp and the Broken Witch suspected nerve damage.

She pulled leaves free and applied them with a coating of

sap, then engaged one of her daggers and pressed it point first into the wound. Makena gargled and the Broken Witch put her other hand over his mouth to silence him. She looked around; the battle crashed and lumbered on, thick with the entwined smells of sweat and exhaustion. No one was paying her and Makena any attention. She looked at him again.

They became lovers after she saved him from a spear injury six months ago, hauling him out of a battle briefer but more intense than this one. He was no looker, but he was charming, and he understood her need to be simultaneously worshipped and dominated. At the next battle, he saved her; stabbing a warrior twice his size who was about to decapitate the Broken Witch as she crouched over yet another casualty, trying and in that case failing to engage the Way sufficiently to affect a recovery. She had needed deep comforting after that, and Makena had been the one to do it.

Now, though, Makena was grey with strain and the Broken Witch had to get him off the field if he was to survive. Unfortunately, a less well-known aspect of the Choice was the relative importance of who should live. Makena was an able warrior, but he was a foot soldier rather than one of the more valuable mounted fighters or archers, who took longer to train and were thus harder to replace.

The Broken Witch looked around at the chaotic horror of hand to hand warfare; the fate of nations decided as always by people in dented armour scrapping in a field. She concluded that Makena was worth it, and that she would do everything she could to get him to the healing camp.

To her right, a horse exploded.

It was hard to see how it happened; the Zabardan horse

and rider were racing through the battle, laying waste to invaders. Suddenly there was a burst of bloody light, then man and beast vanished in a red storm. The scarlet drizzle cleared to reveal a tall man who would be pale if he wasn't drenched in blood. His long, black hair was slick with it, while heat from his red sword made the ruby fluid crack and pop.

Others came at Feros. The red sword flicked, warriors fell; Feros picked up their weapons and hurled them into the bodies of others. The Daxu were strong in him; the Broken Witch could hear their music. It was as beautiful as Feros himself, for all his calm butchery.

For the first time, the Broken Witch was nervous. She looked at Makena, who groaned. Perhaps it would be best to get Makena out of here; forget Feros and…

And then Large Basu would die.

The Broken Witch sat in the heart of battle with no idea what to do. She held Makena tightly, but he had passed out. She looked at Feros again.

He was running at her.

She was so terrified that she dropped Makena, who twitched against the ground. The Broken Witch scrabbled back. She must get her swords! One was next to Makena; she snatched it up, turned and then Feros was on her.

The Vessel of Her Beauty

Was it terror that yanked the Broken Witch back to the village? She stood, halfway across, unable to go any further. The visual storm had passed, perhaps blown away by the power of those repressed memories as they roared up out of the Broken Witch's shocked mind.

She could see the entrance to the cave in the wall ahead, the expanse of ground that kept her from it, and the huts either side. The sun was overhead in its familiar vault of ever-rich blue, a breeze drifted in from the west, lifting the Broken Witch's hair across her shoulders, and everything was horrible.

It was as though goodness and substance had drained away, leaving only shells. The Broken Witch was aground, unable to move. It was not the floppiness she had known in the steam room; it was more a sense of being *locked*.

Desperation didn't work, even though she wanted to get out of the dread as much as she wanted to save Precious Child. Anger didn't work because it blended so easily with the dread. Love didn't work, any more than life could survive the deep desert, where the burning time lasted all day.

A distant patter, red splashes on the ground, and a

swooning sense of dissolution let the Broken Witch know she was bleeding. She could not see where she was bleeding from, and while her flesh was still a thick layer of agony she could not locate or identify a specific wound. Otherwise, the silence was a terrific pressure, her head squeezed by monstrous fingers she could not see, and her body so crushed it seemed smaller.

She tried to move her head, but it was frozen in place. She could not move her eyes. She could not blink. Her jaw was shut tight, as if her teeth had fused. Her body was distant, and inert as a rock.

A weird sound echoed through the eerie layers of tension. It was a low snarl, as if something was near the Broken Witch… No. Something was in her. Had the dread somehow created some living version of itself inside her? The Broken Witch had thought herself numb to future shocks, but the thought of some ghastly formation ripping itself free of her was so horrific she managed to twitch.

She realised that she was hungry.

It shouldn't matter. She did not have far to go, for all that it seemed an eternity, and she had not needed sustenance this far. And yet look how thin her arms had become! Her belly was tight, and her lips felt thin, drawn back as her flesh receded. Such was the energy needed to traverse the dread, the Broken Witch must have burned through the food the Stonesinger's wife brought that morning and begun to digest herself.

This was why she was back in the village, and not in the dubiously merciful distractions of the past. Unable to sustain itself, her body had demanded she return and see to it. The Broken Witch would have been annoyed if she'd had the energy. Instead, she was stranded, with no fuel to continue and no means of getting any.

A spike of rage brought the question of why she had not considered this likelihood before she set out, as though crossing the dread was something lots of people had done, and provided instructions for, which the Broken Witch had not bothered to follow. She managed to recognise that even by her own high standards of absurdity this was a good one, but doing so did not ease that merciless nagging, those recriminations from past and present that she could no more escape than she could take a step forward in the brutal clamp of the dread.

A more pressing concern made itself known. Her eyes had been open in the bright desert air for a while now, and they began to water. Soon her tears would dry in the heat, her eyes would not be lubricated, and the dust and unfiltered sunlight would blind her. A steady beat of panic sped up. She had overcome the visual storm, but she would not recover from permanent damage to her eyes. How would she find Precious Child then?

The dread made it easy for the Broken Witch to subside into self-hate. What a joke she was. Skitting from one thing to another, destroying all in her way. She was so careless it was a kind of stupidity, she who valued her cunning so.

She lacked commitment in everything. Why had she kept her male aspects? Her reasons now seemed trite, indulgent even. She was not a broken witch because something bad had happened in some long-ago war; she was broken because that is what she did with promises, with relationships, with love.

Large Basu was ever-forgiving, ever-understanding, always quiet and kind. How he must have loathed his idiot offspring beneath it all, the way she loathed herself.

That was the wellspring of her promiscuity: a need to blot out self-hate with the intensity of endless brief liaisons, when people who did not know her wanted her to the exclusion of everything else. The power of that, the overwhelming need, was a drug more powerful than any she had experienced.

The dread echoed these awful thoughts and made them deafening. The Broken Witch felt she had been reduced to the size of a grain of sand in the centre of the Realm of Knowing, and these terrible accusations reverberated off the smooth curved walls to hit her like rocks.

She considered ending her struggle right there, letting the dread swamp her until that was all she was. For would it truly be a mercy to save Precious Child? Precious Child was half Broken Witch – how much would that disgusting character come to dominate in the years to come? To what extent had the Broken Witch cursed Precious Child simply by enabling her existence?

Her tears flowed more quickly now, and all she could see was a series of blurs that sharpened the light into needles as it struck her tormented eyes. Even that agony grew dim, for pain takes energy and the Broken Witch had none. Deep within herself she began to come loose, and even the accusing voice grew quiet.

Soon little was left. The Broken Witch became like a sandstone pillar in the deep desert, a place where no person would go. She was not merely alone, she was unregarded. The memory of her would fade until it would be as if she had never lived. Her beauty, her power, her spirit, all were worn away by the wind and the sand, which rose and rose until she was buried. Even then the destruction did not stop, for in the grind of the ever-shifting desert what shape she kept was eroded until nothing remained.

.

..

...

The love of the village is my greatest weapon…

…A little boy who was always solemn and serious, whose leg had bent the wrong way after a fall from climbing the baduba tree… I calmed him with berries and a funny story about an ant that scared off an army led by an idiot simply by not getting out of the way; then, while the boy was distracted, reset the leg faster than the pain could register and distracted him again before he cried out… How the leg healed well, and he always walked properly afterwards and even started to swagger a bit, especially when he was made Headmun…

…A woman who had only known one man, who had never loved another before and never would again, whose love was so intense she did not say much but everyone felt that love regardless… How the husband sickened and would not get better even though I attended him daily and journeyed far for the herbs needed to ease his days… And the woman kept her husband for three more good years she would not have enjoyed if not for me… And she always kept his name instead of her own, so everyone called her the Widow Ndugu…

…A man who sweated and shook in the throes of tinge

fever, his eyes glowing pink and the weird flowery smell of the disease coming off him… Tinge fever can spread by touch, and when a place has no witch, sufferers are banished to protect the rest… I did not care and looked after him anyway, even though only luck prevented me getting the same illness… I gathered food and water and sealed myself in his hut with him and when Adebinte recovered we made love for two days…

…The Stonesinger's wife spread before me in all her beauty, on her back in the bed in the room that my father and I slept in… The Stonesinger kneeling behind me, stroking my hair and my shoulders and then gripping my hips and entering me, the outrageous shock of that, the brief hungry pain and then the deep gratification, his hands on my breasts, his clever fingers tormenting them… The Stonesinger's wife reaching up and drawing me down until I slid into the glorious hot wet press of her, 'We love you, Bambomiyi,' she whispered; 'We love you,' her husband sighed in my ear and I wanted to say 'I love you too,' but her mouth was on mine and then…

···

··

·

The Broken Witch stared down at the bulge in the front of her wrap. Really? *That* was what hauled her back from oblivion?

It made sense, she supposed. The urge to reproduce drove all creatures to the most ridiculous extremes. People were no different; even the Daxu had not been immune to it, as the existence of the Broken Witch demonstrated.

So, she was still alive, but back in the dread, and it was no less awful than before; indeed, its predations were even more overwhelming now the Broken Witch was weaker. Yet the moments free of struggle, when she had unwittingly risked all by giving in, had yielded a brief clarity.

There were huts nearby. They would have food, and they would have water, and all she had to do was reach the nearest one, get inside, eat, drink and be on her way.

The nearest hut was eight steps to her left. She lifted the enormous weight of her leg, shaking with the strain of it, and lowered it; then she lifted the other and swayed. Her breath was fast, and her lungs ached as if she'd run a great distance. This was the most dangerous part of the undertaking; if she fell again, she would not be able to get back up. She got her foot down and allowed herself a moment of triumph, a reminder that she was not as terrible as she thought; that simply because she had got some things wrong did not mean she did not deserve to live. Besides, as she was beginning to realise, some mistakes turn out to be very useful…

Seven more steps to go. She lifted her leg again, and in this manner made her painful way to the hut.

Fortunately, there was no door to negotiate. Instead, the Broken Witch found a string curtain of coloured stones, and started as she recognised her father's handiwork. No one could cast beads like Large Basu; the little spheres were his trademark. The Broken Witch moved through them, as through a cool, tickling constellation of beautiful worlds, each too rich with possibility and wonder to be fully understood in a single life.

Once inside, Broken Witch saw she was in luck: a meal had been laid and then abandoned as the dread closed in. Unfortunately, the table was on the far side of the hut, which the distortions of the dread rendered as a great vault.

Worse still was how an enclosed space focussed the dread. Terrible though the dizzying altered perspectives outside were, they seemed like the safe side of the village compared to the way the dread funnelled itself through the hut, in the same way as those lethal winds were intensified by the carved mountain above the Realm of Knowing.

The Broken Witch could smell the food, and her mouth watered as her enervated senses picked out ingredients. There was duck and tuber stew in a thick berry juice, cold now after standing for a day but still good (indeed, the woodsinger tribe whose recipe it was tended to eat it like that), cakes of fruit and grain seasoned with desert honey, stonesung cups of desert apple wine and, in pride of place at the centre, a smoke pot with four slim inhalation tubes equally spaced around the upper third.

A high-pitched gasp of desire found its way out of the Broken Witch, but again she could not move. It was not a visual storm that obstructed her this time, or the physical predations of the dread. It was merely the quite reasonable unwillingness of a living creature to go any further into an intolerable environment made still worse by restricted space that acted as a grotesque echo chamber.

Her strength began to work against her, as her obstinate mind created impassable barriers. The hut floor became a lake of molten rock, and a single touch of her foot would incinerate her. That such a phenomenon was no more physically dangerous than a mirage was of no consequence. In her desperate exhaustion, the Broken Witch had unconsciously allowed herself to believe it was true. If she took another step her mind would create the necessary physical response, and she would be immolated.

In the meantime, she only had a brief respite from starvation. Lust had got her in here, but now even that primal force had burned itself out. If she didn't move soon, she would shut down and become trapped again.

The Broken Witch found herself thinking of those beads on the curtain as she came in and wondered why. Maybe she had gone properly insane this time, and these scattered thoughts were her last expressions of rationality –

No, no, *no*. She had to stop attacking herself like that. It was as if she had become the dread and was doing its frightful work for it.

She was thinking of those beads for a reason, and it was this: her father had created them, and her father was a practical man whose quiet example had kept the Broken Witch alive more often than any of her engagements with the Way. So: what would Large Basu do?

He would stop trying to get to the table, and instead get the table to come to him.

What?

Again, the Broken Witch questioned her sanity, and then she saw what the food was lying on. It was a woodsung table, a pale yellow, sinuous, gleaming creation of smooth curves and an oval top like the surface of a still pool. While it did not have a fraction of a woodwing's power, the table was still a creation of the Way, and so in theory could act as a temporary vehicle.

Wait, what was she thinking? She had no power; she was broken, and besides, the Kani Paths were outside the village, which meant they might as well be on the other side of Zabardu.

The Broken Witch wondered why she was accepting limitations now of all times. She knew she would not survive the dread, that she was here for her beloved village and for Precious Child in particular, so why not, at least, try?

Slowly, as though lifting the entire hut, she raised her hand, so her palm pointed at the table. Her other hand she spread in the direction of the Kani Paths. She pictured that crossroads in the desert, the old beaten path that bisected the better-maintained one, the debris along the sides, the stone markers. For a moment she saw the Kani Paths as they appeared to her before she was broken: corridors of power that glowed brighter than the desert sun as they stretched up into the sky like thick, translucent walls that struck through the dazzling landscape.

The table did not move.

It was not surprising. The Broken Witch had only moments before she collapsed, and she would not have been able to engage the Way even if she was not being horribly reduced by the dread.

She would kill for that duck stew though…

The Broken Witch did not sag or give any other indication that she had quit. Instead, she recalled the Realm of Knowing, and how those bright silver seeds had sifted themselves through her, bringing energy and information… Bringing it to a fertile place, a rich environment… The oasis that was Basu, who was Large Basu's precious child, confused but proud descendent of the mighty Daxu.

Still the table did not move.

The Broken Witch knew that if she did not get that food inside her in the next five seconds, she would be dead.

There is a special genius that people find in moments of ultimate peril, when all distractions have been sheared away, all choices made, and when all the pointlessly critical voices have fallen silent. The Broken Witch realised that she had accessed the past not just via recovered memory, but because her relationship with time was realigned. The bargain with Thema, the battle, the approach of Feros – all were more than recollections, they had somehow happened both in the past and in the journey through the dread.

Instead of trying to do something impossible now, perhaps the Broken Witch could access her past self, who would have found such a task easy.

As the dread continued its ferocious work upon her, the Broken Witch's consciousness contracted. She saw, as if she was standing on a darkened world, a bright gold weave all about her. It seemed familiar, and she realised that the world pattern of the Kani Paths was replicated in her mind, and that it would always be there whether she was broken or not. No part of it could be subtracted without collapsing the whole, but if she just took a few glimmers of brightness from there, and a few from there, and a few from *there…*

*

Twenty-two years earlier, she fell with her woodwing from the mile-high tree whose seed she had woven it from. This was their first flight together after it tasted her blood, and the one that would spell the end of both if the woodwing didn't activate the engagement that would link it to the Kani Path and enable flight. The Broken Witch could do nothing but trust, her power not needed for the first half second they plunged towards the distant forest floor, so the pulse her future-self borrowed was not even needed, and hidden in the panic of descent…

Making love with Lusala in a tent on a savanna plain the day before a battle, the two kazo had enhanced their sensual perceptions with a mixture of milk liqueur that had implausibly survived the journey north; a burning root the Broken Witch had heard about but never found until yesterday whose fumes transformed the tent into a smoky realm of endless possibility; and a series of engagements triggered by pricking each other's flesh in patterns that activated one after the other. Doing so amplified the effects of liqueur, the rich, thrilling root smoke, and their own intense desire into a journey so powerful that when one point failed to ignite because its power had been snatched into the future, neither kazo noticed…

Aged seven, little Basu sat in the living room and was surprised to see her father come in from the workshop, the back of his hand bleeding. He had dropped a stonesung pot and instinctively tried to catch it, forgetting how heavy the thing was until the last moment, when even snatching his hand away was not enough to prevent the breaking pieces slicing him above the knuckle. Large Basu almost never got angry, but today he was flustered because his work would be doubly delayed by replacing the stonesung pot and now the inconvenience of injury, and it was for the cattle tribe who were only here for another few hours and would not be back for months… Little Basu reached up and held her father's hand, and the blood stopped and then the wound closed. Large Basu gasped and snatched his hand away – not in horror, for his big face opened with delight at the discovery of his child's gift, but because she used too much power and smudged his flesh into a perfectly circular scar that he never let her get rid of. There was enough of the Way aglow in that moment for a spark to be employed elsewhere, in another time…

*

Showing off to Makena as the Zabardan army approached the great grassy plain where their fates would be settled, she flew her woodwing high along the Kani Path. Silly Makena was scared of heights and trembled delightfully in the Broken Witch's arms whenever she described the feel of soaring above everything. She knew he would groan yet be unable to stop watching as the Broken Witch ascended until she grew icy cold and had to use an engagement to carry on breathing, then went higher until the blue of the sky faded into a lush and terrifying inky black and the stars came out even though it was day. She could see so much of Zabardu it was almost possible to cover it with the hand she extended over that intolerable, unthinkable drop. There was a moment when she remembered she was not a bird, and that maybe she ought not to be up here after all, a moment whose power was needed far in the future, a moment forgotten almost at once…

The moments gathered into the present, seeding themselves in the Broken Witch like musical notes, opening and spreading until the great chorus emerged…

In the hut in the village the table did not move, but that no longer mattered. The table was aglow with all the power of the Broken Witch's life, and the food and the smoke pot herbs had evaporated into a glittering cloud that flowed across the miles of burning floor so she could inhale it. The table had been set for eight, and this great volume of nourishing goodness rushed into the Broken Witch.

The dread had drained and damaged her with fearsome speed, but The Broken Witch used the power of the remembered Way to match the dread with life-giving ferocity. Nourishment wove together her damaged flesh, and knitted strength into her brittle bones. She found movement easier and shook her head, her hair rustling down her back. The herbs in the smoke pot pushed away the self-doubt and loathing. They gave her a perspective to counter the dread, which in its very remorselessness became a simple force to be deflected.

The Broken Witch took a deep breath, turned and walked from the hut. Her goal was ahead of her, but already her strength began to fade, her hard-earned resilience wilting. She was halfway through her journey, and she suspected she would be as diminished when she reached her destination as she had been when she entered the hut.

Then the past gathered around her once again, bringing with it a brief respite, and the promise of a truth as devastating as the dread.

A Chase in the Sky

Feros was a head taller than the Broken Witch and broader too, while his red sword was three times the length of her white ones. He jabbed at her and she could sense the weapon's power; knew that even the setatu would not protect her this time. The Broken Witch leaped aside and snatched her other sword from its sheath.

Feros moved faster than a big man should be able to. His face was calm, and the Broken Witch felt pitiful against him. The red sword came down with a speed that cut the air; a discord in the Way that only Feros and the Broken Witch could hear.

The Broken Witch got her two swords up and parried the blow, but the force of it almost knocked her to her knees. However, Feros had left his middle exposed and the Broken Witch got a good kick in, sending Feros back, bent double. The Broken Witch batted the red sword aside and attacked with both swords in two directions. Feros could only parry one; the other went into his side and he fell to one knee.

The Broken Witch pressed her advantage with a crazed flurry of cuts; again, Feros managed to parry some of them, but a third got through. His blood flowed freely now. He tried to raise his sword, but it was clearly too much for him. The Broken Witch prepared the killing blow.

She hesitated.

From above, something dark appeared. The Broken Witch realised two things: one was that Thema's strategy had worked and the battle had moved onto the south west Kani Paths; two: another kazo approached, but this one was the enemy.

The other kazo was on them before the Broken Witch could kill Feros. The Broken Witch did not even get a good look at her; there was only the sense of a very tall, slim woman with flowing black hair and huge eyes. She was less pale than the others, her skin the colour of dark honey. Her setatu was an iridescent dark blue, and her woodwing a sleek airborne tree whose leaves were every shade of green.

Something struck the Broken Witch in the chest and knocked her back; she looked down and saw a bone dagger embedded just beneath her heart. She pulled it out, freed one of her own and pressed it into the wound. Her reactions were instinctively quick, but the Broken Witch still felt the cold spread of an enemy engagement in her blood. She sagged to the ground.

She thought of Makena and looked around for him but could see only bodies. Suddenly exhausted, the Broken Witch struggled with the enemy engagement. She knew most poisons; it was just a question of calculating, remembering… Ah, yes, there it was.

Her eyes cleared in time to see the other kazo kneel before Feros with her back to him. She used handles on her back-mounted swords to hook into loops on the front of

Feros's dark red leathern armour. When the woman stood, her strength was such that she could lift the big man almost without effort. The Broken Witch got a good look at the other kazo and almost forgot to complete the engagement.

The woman was beyond beautiful. Although young, she had a queenly aspect that spoke of exquisite breeding. Her olive skin gleamed with martial sweat and her long, black hair rippled as she moved towards her woodwing. From the grace of her motion to the song of her power, it was clear the Daxu were even stronger in her than they were in Feros.

I want to be you, the Broken Witch thought.

The other kazo glanced at the Broken Witch, then mounted her woodwing with Feros on her back and was up and gone.

The Broken Witch staggered to her feet and managed to get both swords back in their sheaths. She summoned her own woodwing, which looped up in the distance and raced around the Kani Paths towards her.

As it approached, she thought of Makena again. She could still save him. She could still save herself. But she could not do that and save Large Basu.

The woodwing dropped beside her.

She mounted it and soared up over the battle.

The other kazo was a black mark in the sky ahead: small and getting smaller. The Broken Witch flew along the Kani Path in pursuit, aiming to get close enough to hurl a dagger through Feros and finish him. The Broken Witch did not want to fight the other kazo, who she feared more than the warrior.

The gap between them closed as the Broken Witch engaged the Way more fully. The woodwing sank its thorns into her wrists and sucked more blood to maintain the link between them. The Broken Witch barely noticed.

As the Way surged through her she heard an overpowering, unearthly music, its intensity a deep echo like an itch in the mind. The Broken Witch felt the air rush against her bared teeth as she went after the other woodwing. Details of her quarry became clear again: the big man dripping blood onto the floor of the Kani Path far below; the dark banner of the other woman's hair as it flowed behind her, the curve of her long legs.

The kazo was heading for the coast, although the Broken Witch did not know of any invader bases there. She pulled her two swords from their sheaths on her back and held them out either side of her, edges into the wind. She arranged the most complex engagement she had ever attempted, to gain more speed. The blades glowed and golden patterns flowed behind her sight.

The music of the Way was deafening now, but the Broken Witch did not stop. She would save Large Basu and end the war as well. She would save everybody! They would all love her, everyone in the village, the invaders, the gorgeous woman on the woodwing ahead – what a couple they would make! Nothing could stop them!

I CAN STOP YOU.

"What? Who –?" the Broken Witch stuttered.

YOU CANNOT KILL FEROS.

"I can! I will!"

I WILL NOT ALLOW IT.

"Ha!"

USE YOUR MIND TO SPEAK TO ME.

How do I do that?

YOU ARE DOING IT NOW.

Oh. Are you the other kazo?

KAZO?

On the woodwing ahead.

THE WITCH? NO.

Who are you, then?

IT WOULD BE BEST IF YOU NEVER FOUND OUT.

I shall be the judge of that, thank you. And I will kill Feros.

FEROS IS THE BROTHER OF OUR KING. HE IS OF GREAT VALUE TO US.

Why should I care? You are invaders! You are the enemy!

SADLY, YES.

The Broken Witch shook her head.

My father will die if I do not complete this mission.

GO AND SAVE HIM THEN.

The price for desertion is torture, imprisonment and execution.

SO?

I –

The Broken Witch flew on, her mind in turmoil.

YOU ARE BASU, ARE YOU NOT?

Yes.

BASU, PLEASE TURN ASIDE.

No.

YOU ARE OF THE WAY. THERE ARE FEWER AND FEWER OF US. DO NOT MAKE ME DESTROY YOU.

You cannot! Feel how strong I am!
**YOU BURDEN YOURSELF IN THIS PURSUIT,
MORE THAN YOU REALISE.**
You are not real!
I ASSURE YOU I AM.
You are just a voice in my head!
TURN ASIDE.

The Broken Witch could see the coast ahead, where the cliffs ended far above the sea. The other kazo dropped off the cliff edge and disappeared. The Broken Witch pursued her and saw two ships far below in the bay. The kazo and Feros headed towards the farthest, and the other began moving to intercept the Broken Witch.

Something flashed on its deck and the Broken Witch felt the weapon's passage burn her cheek. She gathered the power she had accumulated in the pursuit, which was becoming increasingly difficult to manage, and pointed both her swords at the attacking ship. She altered the engagement and discharged power at the vessel, seeing it rock in the water as a large piece of it broke off and crashed into the sea.

The ship began to list, and the Broken Witch closed on the other kazo and Feros again. The two swords she had used in the engagement were burned down to white stubs, so the Broken Witch hurled them aside and pulled out her side swords. She only needed to get another twenty feet.

The other kazo began evasive manoeuvres of such skill that the Broken Witch had to re-sheath her swords to control the woodwing and keep up. They swooped across the sea and in and out of the ships' upper structures.

The vessels were so huge they could only have been made

by the Daxu. The Broken Witch had a moment to marvel at the scale before more flashes cracked off deck-mounted mirrors. The woodwing shuddered at the impact; the Broken Witch engaged the Way to ensure sap flowed to douse any flames, then got out of range. However, the woodwing was sluggish and the Broken Witch despaired as the other kazo began to draw away.

The Broken Witch pulled out her swords again and engaged the Way even more fully, her mind a whirl of calculation and her body tight with energy. The woodwing groaned at the power being forced through it, but the Broken Witch was focused solely on running a sword through Feros's back.

The setatu Sila was hot around her, normal temperature adjustments no longer functioning. It did not matter, because once more the Broken Witch was closing on her quarry. Twenty feet, fifteen, ten…

Out of the sun came something vast and golden.

The Broken Witch could not quite make out what it was; she had no frame of reference for it or understanding of how such a thing could be. It flew without using a Kani Path and its size should have prevented it from ever getting airborne. It did not move like a bird but glided through the sky as if controlling gravity itself.

There was a feeling of great age about it. The Broken Witch could tell this being had come from the Daxu, that it had even known them.

Mournful golden eyes moved on either side of the streamlined head, while the sleek, gleaming body moved with absolute, terrifying grace. The limbs were like fronds and ended in strange, diamond shapes that seemed to conjure power from the very fabric of reality.

Five feet.

BASU.

That great voice again.

The last warning.

Two feet: the sword out.

One foot.

And –

One Country Made of Love

"Fourteen years ago, I woke by the wreck in the desert," the Broken Witch told the dread. "I remember what the wreck is now. It is that piece of the great ship I broke off, just before…"

She took a shuddering breath.

"The great golden sky beast burned the power from me, burned my woodwing, burned my setatu, burned the hair from my head. The other kazo, the 'witch', gave me some of hers, and that is why it looks like this now."

The dread whirled about, indifferent.

"The sky beast sent me back here through some unknowable route and used the wrecked piece of ship to protect me. That journey destroyed my memories, so I would never be able to do it again.

"And when I got here, Large Basu had died and gone into the under-waters. I never even got to hold him."

Her tears fell through the dread onto the rock.

The dread churned through it all, silent and overwhelming, its nauseating despair like a spreading infection.

The Broken Witch looked up. She saw that in her reverie

she had passed to the other side of the village but felt no sense of triumph. Why, after all, had she gone north to fight in the first place? She had a talent for combat, as much as for healing; it was why she was an ideal kazo, but the decision to join the war had still been hers.

Could it be that she desperately wanted to prove her worth?

Hard to say now, and it no longer mattered. The Broken Witch hauled herself up and through the opening into the cave.

"Precious Child!" she called.

Despite her feast in the hut, the Broken Witch had once again lost a third of her body weight completing her quest across the village. Her sultry muscularity was gone, and her inelegant limbs were like sticks. Her hair felt wispy. Her breasts sagged. She got turned around in the dread and saw another spattered blood trail behind her. It was still unclear where she was bleeding from. The Broken Witch turned her back on the blood and staggered on.

The dread magnified her heartbeat, so it sounded like the blows of a hammer in her chest and head. She realised how much pain she was in and tried to ignore it, but the dread boosted the pain and no rationale or bloody-mindedness worked against it.

"Precious Child!"

Already distorted by the dread, there was also a new and unwelcome rasp in the Broken Witch's voice. The Broken Witch had heard that tone many times before, in dying men and women.

Somehow, she went on, ignoring the desperate calls of her drained body to stop for a moment and rest. There was no sense in burning out again. Why not sleep?

"Because I will not wake up, Dread," the Broken Witch whispered.

At the top of the stairs leading down to the algae ponds, the Broken Witch realised she would have to go down in a sitting position, like a very young child. She had to concede the wisdom of it; if she fell, she would not survive the impact.

Painfully, she went down, and each step was harder than the last. At the bottom, she knelt. Bloody sweat dripped from her. She could sense the cool presence of the algae pond nearby, but the dread was down here, too.

"Bambomiyi!"

It was another voice from the past. A child's. Whose –?

"Bambomiyi! Over here!"

The Broken Witch lifted the intolerable weight of her head and gazed over the algae pond.

Across the green-coated expanse there was a curved rock shelf next to the fat square of the pond raft, which lay still on the quiet water. A five-year-old girl in a battered lion outfit jumped up and down on the shelf and waved.

"It is safe here, Bambomiyi!" Precious Child shouted. "Pull yourself over with the skimming ropes."

The Broken Witch toppled forward into the water.

There was no dread beneath the surface.

It was like feeling the sun's warmth after a freezing desert night, or drinking after a great thirst, or another's touch after a long period alone. The Broken Witch hung in the cool, dark green, then opened her eyes and gazed up through the murky water. She would rather drown than be overwhelmed by the dread again.

Love for Precious Child sent the Broken Witch surging through the surface, prepared to scream her defiance. However, the dread pressed upon her and choked off all sound before she could make it.

It was so hard to simply exist! How did the living creatures of the world manage it, this constant generation of energy? The industry involved merely in being was so unreasonable as to make the inhalation of a single breath more difficult than the greatest construction of the Daxu.

"Bambomiyi!" Precious Child called.

Her voice was like the music of the Way, cutting through the crude horror of the dread like a dazzling light through darkness.

The Broken Witch knew from the time it took to haul herself through the algae pond how little of her great strength remained. She often stopped to rest and sink beneath the surface. Each time, it got harder to come up again.

Little by little she managed it, drawn by the sight of the small girl in her lion outfit; the flash of teeth in dark skin as she smiled, and the crease of worry on her brow as the Broken Witch faltered, lost her grip on the rope and then somehow found it again.

Her fingers touched rock and a tiny hand grabbed the multi-coloured wrap. The Broken Witch found just enough energy to get onto the ledge and –

She woke an unknown time later, a small warm shape against her side. The Broken Witch mumbled, and the shape moved.

"Bambomiyi," Precious Child said. "You slept for *ages*."

"Long day," the Broken Witch managed.

Her voice sounded very strange, as if raw from screaming. Her throat hurt, but the rest of her body was numb. She did not even feel the cold of the water.

Precious Child leaned over the Broken Witch with that perfect balance of profound concern for another and unapologetic self-interest that is the preserve of all five-year olds.

"Why are your eyes bleeding, Bambomiyi?"

"Is that where the blood came from?" the Broken Witch said.

"Not just there," Precious Child said, but did not elaborate.

"We must go to the safe side of the village."

"Yes."

Precious Child looked over the immobile bulk of the Broken Witch at the expanse of green-coated water.

"Um…" she began.

"I will think of something," the Broken Witch said. "We have food and water and…"

She remembered how the dread was growing; wondered how long they had before it engulfed them here too, and then passed out again.

She woke to the sound of retching and crying. Precious Child was backed against the wall, her eyes wide.

"Did you try and cross?" the Broken Witch said.

Precious Child nodded.

"The dread will destroy you, Precious Child," the Broken Witch said. "Do not try it again."

"But Bambomiyi, you are hurt."

"I have been hurt before. I have got better before."

"You are so thin."

"I am thin because I wish to be; it brings out the fine structure of my bones."

"You always look lovely, Bambomiyi."

"Yes. Thank you, though."

"What shall we do?"

Stripped of everything, the Broken Witch found thought surprisingly easy.

"Did I ever tell you about the great golden sky beast?" she said.

"No," Precious Child replied.

"He was the most beautiful, terrifying creature I have ever seen."

"More than the lions?"

"Yes," the Broken Witch said. "They don't fly, for a start."

"More than the elephants?" Precious Child said.

"He had something of the elephants about him – their great size, power and wisdom. But greater than them, yes."

"I can barely imagine such a thing."

"To see him was…"

The Broken Witch managed to shake her head.

"He took my power from me. He did not want to do it. He did his duty as I was doing mine. He could have killed me and did not; indeed, he and his companion, who was a witch like I am, went to great efforts to save me. Why did they do that, I wonder?

"Could they in some fashion have known what was to occur here in the village? From the feel of his voice in my head, I could tell the sky beast had a strange manner of seeing; that normal time did not mean to him what it means to you and me. Does that make sense, Precious Child?"

"Instead of going from morning to night it goes sideways."

"Exactly that," the Broken Witch said. "You are a clever girl."

"Yes," Precious Child said, and the Broken Witch laughed.

"This dread," the Broken Witch said. "I will not survive trying to cross it again and you certainly will not. But I got this far by remembering how I came to be broken and I think, somehow, I remembered it all for a reason, as if it is a clue."

The Broken Witch reached a shaky hand into the water, formed a cup with her palm and lifted the hand out again. A little pool rippled there.

"I am like this hand. The dread is like the water."

"You will take it into you?"

"Yes."

"Will it hurt?"

"I do not know."

"If it hurts will you do it anyway?"

"Yes."

"Will you die?"

"I hope not, if only so that I can finish the task."

"Do not die, Bambomiyi. I love you so very much."

"I love you too, Precious Child."

"You are my other mother and my other father."

"You know that truth?"

"I have always known it."

"Good. It is important to know where you came from."

Precious Child leaned over and kissed the Broken Witch's lips. The Broken Witch smiled.

She did not think. She did not prepare. She merely recognised herself as she was at that moment, fully.

She knew the many levels of her life and her power; she saw Large Basu nearby, as vivid as if he was standing there. She saw the village, from above, below and both sides. She saw the wreck.

She remembered now how the sky beast had broken her, with a great cry of grief; how the sky beast missed the Daxu, how he loved all their descendants equally regardless of sides in a petty war. She remembered the feeling of it, the sundering, the burning – oh, the burning. The horror of fire, the terror of it; this unreasonable, barely controllable thing.

And yet as she flew across the water of the algae pond, leaving Precious Child behind, the Broken Witch remembered the journey across Zabardu fourteen years ago; a blazing pathway through the very stuff of the world, the fabric of sky and star with only the fragment of a Daxu ship to protect her. That journey had opened something in her; some new means of perception, forgotten until now.

The Broken Witch turned it upon the dread and the dread entered her like a lover.

There was reluctance; she could hear screaming but was not certain if it was her, the dread or all people from all times when they reach this point. There was also a great, deep pleasure from the cosmic source: a sense of totality, a perfection beyond the reach of time.

She was aware of fighting up the stairs as if through a storm; ribbons of darkness around her, a ferocious pull on her wasted muscles. It was like a cloud of sticky, black matter whose fibres yanked at her, their purpose an expression of supreme resistance.

The Broken Witch recognised sunlight in her eyes as she

forced her way through the impossible space on the empty side of the village. She felt laughter within her, a deeper laughter than she had ever known. The dread was not inert; it was joining itself with her to form something else.

The rocky ground of the village wore away the tough skin of her soles as she forced her way on. She felt the pain of raw skin against rough stone, but it didn't matter. The pain quickly became something else: a new sound, outside the Way. Oh, beautiful!

Her strength came back, and it was greater than before. It no longer mattered that the Way was lost to her; it was merely part of the entirety she was becoming; that of which beauty is a mortal reflection.

The dread rushed from the village into the Broken Witch and she welcomed and took it all. Each breath brought more of it, a colossal influx of potential. She waved her arms as if dancing, pulling the dread in, *come! Be one with me!*

She was at the edge of the village now; the great opening and brilliant desert before her. How astonishing it was!

She was aware of people behind her filling the whole village once more: Togo and the Widow Ndugu, the Headmun and the cattle man. Precious Child ran up out of the caves to the Stonesinger and his wife, who gathered the little girl up and swung her about, their joy a surge of brightness.

It was easy, now.

Run, Broken Witch.

So, she did, out of the village with the dread within her, across the desert to the crossroads of the Kani Paths.

Run, Bambomiyi.

So, she did, there at the cross: the meeting, as she herself was a meeting between human and Daxu, man and woman, warrior and healer, inspiration and dread.

Run, Basu.

So, she did, there at the heart of the eight-pointed star; no longer running across the sand but up, up and beyond, the song of the dread transformed within her; up into the air over the desert, up into the dark blue sky towards the racing moon and dancing stars.

At the same time, she ran down: down into the sand, its gentle caress warm and then cool, covering her, the last strands of her hair slipping under and gone, dropping through the rocky aeons and the burning lakes that raged in supple glory; down, down through the metal echoes and the voice of time to the sweet heart of a new sun.

Discover Luna Novella in our store: